Marooned

(A prequel to the Arcadia's Children Series)

By
Andrew R Williams

Andrew R Williams

Dedication

To Tom, Beryl, Colin, Peggy and Vic: Gone but not forgotten.

Thank You

Liam at Akom Creative Ltd – for the cover artwork
Emma at The Word Hutt Publishing

The Author

Some legends say that Andrew R Williams travelled to Earth from a dying world thousands of years ago to share the stories of his home planet. Others say that he is nothing more than a brain in a jar, slowly using his telepathic probes to take control of the planet.

All of them were wrong.....The truth is that Andrew is a retired Chartered Surveyor. He dreams of adventuring through the stars—travelling through worlds filled with thrilling adventure, nightmare creatures, psychotic A.I. and a pet Pterodactyl.

And now, thanks to the invention of the quill pen. Andrew has managed to bring these worlds to all of us.

And now we can all join in.

Other books by Andrew R Williams: Science Fiction

Arcadia's Children (Samantha's Revenge) ISBN 978-1-61309-710-6 (also in ebook)
Arcadia's Children 2: The Fyfield Plantation ISBN 978-1-61309-630-7 (also in ebook)
Arcadia's Children 3: Pushley's Escape ISBN 979-8-65513-597-0 (also in ebook)
Arcadia's Children 4: Exodus ISBN 978-1-91631-243-2 (also in ebook)

Arcadia's Children 5: Samantha's War ISBN 978-1-91631-248-7 (also in ebook)

Superior Action Sci-Fi ISBN 978-1-91631-249-4
Novel (Action Thriller) Jim's Revenge: ISBN ISBN-10: 1916312411 ISBN-13: 978-1916312418

Technical Books

Technical Domestic Building Surveys: ISBN 0 419 178000 7 (also in ebook)
 Spons Practical Guide to Alterations and Extension ISBN 10: 0-415-43426-2 (also in ebook)

Web Links:
https://arwilliamsgateway.com
 https://www.amazon.co.uk/Andrew-R.-Williams/e/B001HPK7KK
https://www.arcadiaschildren.com/
http://www.authorsden.com/andrewrwilliams

Preface

Mary Klempers heard the doorbell ring. She moved towards a blister window and glanced out. Her heart immediately sank because she could see a police car parked below. Pulling back from the window in case she was seen, Mary rushed out of the kitchen and into the small lounge and gasped, "It's the police."

Rob Kinfrank gave her a sharp look and said, "Go into our bedroom and hide under the bed. ***And keep quiet***."

A few seconds later, there was a ring on the bell; Rob Kinfrank calmly walked to the door and activated the intercom. After pushing a button to allow the police access, Kinfrank let out a mild curse and kicked a pair of Mary's slippers under a chair.

A minute later, the lift arrived, and two officers came to the door. One was still wearing his environmental helmet. The other had removed his helmet and had replaced it with an ***I've-got-bad-news face***.

After checking he was at the correct address and speaking to the right person, Bad News said, "Can we come in, sir?"

After allowing both officers in, Kinfrank wrung his hands and said, "Is there something the matter, officers?"

Bad News put his face into words, "I'm afraid there has been an accident, sir."

"Accident! What sort of accident?"

"I'm afraid your wife's body was found in a car in Sector 25 of the Valles Marineris," Bad News replied.

"No!"

"I'm afraid so," Bad News replied. "Your son is alive but very poorly."

"My son's alive!"

"Yes," Bad News replied, "Injured but still alive."

After providing details of the son's general condition and of the hospital looking after the crash victim, Bad News said, "There was another fatality, a male of about your age was also in the car."

Kinfrank made no attempt to disguise the truth, "My wife left me over a year ago. She ran off with another man, officer."

After he'd provided information about his wife's new lover, the two officers asked him if he could identify the bodies at the mortuary and then left.

Once the two officers had driven off, Kinfrank walked into the bedroom and told Mary she could come out of hiding. He explained what had happened.

Mary gulped, "Does this mean we won't be able to leave on the Empress of Incognita."

Kinfrank said, "No. We will still be leaving. I'm not hanging around on Mars for a day longer than necessary. Once Mars signs the new extradition laws, I'm cooked."

"But what about Bee Bee, your son?"

Kinfrank's lip curled, "As long as he's well enough to travel, it looks like we will have to take him with us."

Noting the expression on Mary's face, Kinfrank said, "Don't worry, I'll play happy families until we reach the Kepler-452 system."

Chapter One

The Empress of Incognita Hits a Mine

Hello, diary, I'm back.

My arrival started as it usually did. I was flying upwards, and on all sides, bony arms and hands were reaching out to claim me; I could tell they wanted my soul.

As I continued to rise through the strange dark pyramid, a bright light appeared at the top, and more bony arms and hands reached out as if desperate to grab me before I reached the light.

My mother's face appeared. I could tell that she was trying to tell me something because her lips were moving, but I couldn't hear what she was trying to say. Then her face disappeared, and the old dream, the one that had haunted me for months, returned.

I was no longer flying upwards. I was falling, falling, falling down.

Okay, I hear you say, a standard falling dream, except mine always ended the same way. Before I hit bottom, I saw an image of my father, and he was laughing as if amused by my predicament.

I heard his voice, but it seemed far away, and I couldn't understand what he was saying. Then my mind cleared, and I realised what was happening to me; I was coming out of suspension.

God, how I hate coming out of suspension!

I must have moved because a reassuring voice called out, "Are you awake Bee Bee?"

It was my stepmother's voice.

My alias, by the way (not my real name), is James Kinfrank, I'm fifteen years old, nearly sixteen, and I have a smart-talk editor on my tablet to help me write this. I also keep a handwritten diary that contains more personal secrets. One other thing you should know is that people call me Bee Bee, but I'm not going to tell you why because it's embarrassing.

"Are you awake, Bee Bee?"

On the second time of asking, I said, "Yeah, I'm awake, Mary."

If you think it's impertinent of me to call my step-mum Mary, she prefers it that way. She's a lot younger than Dad and very conscious that no one can replace my late mother, and I think she wants me to look upon her as an older friend.

While I was lying there recovering, a powerful light shone through one of the portholes as a repair droid went about its business in the darkness of deep space. The beam split, diffracted by the glazing and began creating light fairies on the ceiling. While my eyes were still following one particular 'fairy', it lit up an empty recovery bunk.

As Dad's unexplained absences had started to worry me, I extracted my tablet and activated it. I checked the history and discovered what I'd suspected. My tablet had been turned on shortly after I had gone into suspension.

A few taps later, Dad's craggy face appeared on the screen, but he didn't seem to realise that he'd triggered the trap I'd set for him. As there was a precise date/time mark in one corner of the recording, there could be little doubt that Dad had been checking up on me while I was in suspension. I'd caught him in the act!

As his face continued to stare out at me, his pale blue eyes seemed to bite into my soul as if trying to discover my innermost secrets.

Feeling uncomfortable even though it was just a photo, I closed down his image, began carrying out other checks, and swiftly realised that Dad had gone through everything.

As I finally turned my tablet off, I began questioning myself. Why did Dad keep checking up on me? Did he think that the surgeons had failed to put me back together correctly? Did he think that I'd become some sort of deviant? And why wasn't Dad in suspension like the rest of us?

I was tempted to say something to Mary, but I shelved the idea because I knew it would cause trouble. Accusing Dad of invading my privacy would stir up a hornet's nest. My relationship with my Dad had been icy for some time, and I didn't want things to worsen.

The mental self-questioning started again, and I wondered if Dad held me responsible for my mother's death.

While I was still deep in thought, Mary called out again, "You're very quiet, Bee Bee. Anything wrong?"

After sliding my tablet back into my bag, I said, "I'm fine."

But then, I couldn't resist asking, "Where's Dad?"

"You know he always recovers from suspension long before we do," Mary replied matter of factly. "He went out early but popped his head in and spoke to me a few minutes ago. He's gone to an important meeting. He asked me to stay with you until you recovered."

That was why I'd heard Dad's voice in my dream. I must have overheard him talking to Mary when he came back. Eventually, I asked, "What sort of meeting?"

"The ship has been involved in a collision," Mary replied.

"A collision!"

Mary turned a light on and smiled, "Don't look so worried, Bee Bee. Your Dad says we're quite safe. The Empress is a big ship, and I don't think the collision is serious."

Eventually, she threw her legs over the side of her recovery bunk and said, "Come on, Bee Bee. We need to go."

As I followed Mary's example, I glanced at her and felt slightly worried. Mary had always been like a stick insect, painfully thin. She seemed even skinner when she came out of suspension. The process also made Mary's skin appear translucent. Now, you could see her veins. From what I've noticed, I could tell that Dad didn't like the changes.

Of course, the ship's water and chemical additives restrictions didn't help either. Before we'd set off, Mary had started to dye her hair blonde to please Dad. According to her, gentlemen preferred blondes, and my Dad was no exception. Unfortunately, the water restrictions on the Empress of Incognita had left Mary with a wide brown band at the parting, and the spray-on touch-up dyes she had with her didn't seem to work correctly.

"Come on, Bee Bee. We need to go."

"Where are we going?"

"To our apartment, of course," Mary replied.

"But what about the collision?" I objected. "Surely we need to go to a secure location?"

"I told you," Mary replied. "The collision wasn't serious, so we're going to our apartment."

I'd better explain. It wasn't really *our* apartment because we shared it with five other families.

As with all starships, the Empress of Incognita couldn't produce enough food to cater for all the passengers and crew at once, so passengers spent most of their journey locked in a suspension unit.

Apartment 10/25 was a bit like a cosmic timeshare; when the other five families were in suspension, Apartment 10/25 was ours. One of the other five families took possession when we were in recess.

As I stood up, my legs rebelled because I'd not used them for several weeks. After stagger-walking to one of the main lifts, we went to the tenth deck. From there, to Apartment 10/25.

After opening the front door, Mary let out a clicking noise with her tongue. One glance around the living space was enough for me to realise the problem. Mary was a cleanliness fanatic, but the Whistons, the previous occupants, hadn't bothered to clean and tidy before they went back into suspension. The slobs had left dirty plates, and cutlery strewed around everywhere.

Mary began to gripe. "This is beyond a joke. They do this deliberately."

As she took dated photographs with her phone, I guessed they were for her complaint to the ship's accommodation department. Unfortunately, the more Mary complained, the more the Whistons increased their awkwardness; in fact, I think the Whistons took great delight in winding her up. The Whistons were the type of people you wouldn't want as permanent neighbours.

Mary cleared away the used crockery and placed it in a dishwasher—then went to our store cupboard and unlocked it. Her tongue clicked again, "The Whistons have been in here."

"How d'you know?"

Mary held up her phone and showed me a dated photograph. She said, "Have a look now."

One glance was enough to prove she was right. The dated picture displayed neatness, but now it was a jumble. As Mary began taking more photographs, I said, "You do realise the Whistons will deny using our stuff. They'll just say it was broken into by one of the other families who live here when we're in suspension."

While we were still discussing what to do about the Whistons, the front door opened, and my Dad came in. After giving me a perfunctory smile, Dad and Mary hugged. As I didn't like PDAs, I inwardly cringed and just said, "Hi, Dad."

Once the clinch had broken up, Mary began complaining about the Whistons, and Dad said he'd deal with it. However, the tone of his voice indicated he'd just conveniently forget and kick the issue into the long grass. The Whiston's were bad news, and it was apparent that Dad didn't want trouble. In any case, I could tell he had more important things on his mind.

His lacklustre reaction was enough to remind Mary where he'd been. "So, how bad was the collision?"

Dad gave Mary a strange half-grin, "As I told you before, nothing to worry about.

No significant damage done, no one killed or injured."

When the strange half-grin remained fixed to his craggy face, Mary said, "What aren't you telling us?"

"This is hush-hush," Dad replied, "So don't go blabbing. It looks like the ship collided with a mine."

Mary's jaw dropped, "Is this one of your jokes?"

"No kidding, the ship hit a mine," my Dad replied. "Carl Whyler, one of the ship's crew, told me."

"Then why are you grinning like a Cheshire Cat?" Mary demanded.

I knew because I'd seen that look on Dad's face before. When we'd lived at Mars Base 5, before my real Mum died, Dad had dragged me out of bed in the early hours of the morning. After telling me to dress, he transported me over fifteen kilometres across rough terrain just to watch a fire that had broken out at the local spaceport.

No doubt we would have stayed there for ages watching the leaping flames, but a police patrol car came over and moved Dad and all the other rubberneckers away. I think Dad would have driven away and turned back, but he saw the officer taking the car registration numbers. Knowing that going back could have resulted in a court appearance and a hefty fine, Dad abandoned his vigil.

On the way home, we skirted along a small section of the Valles Marineris, a deep rift in Mars' surface that stretched for thousands of kilometres. I recall Dad telling me that there had been several fatal accidents in the area when cars had gone over the edge. Some incidents were genuine accidents, but most were suicides.

According to Dad, suicides were widespread on Mars. With some small settlements being so isolated, cabin fever drove some people to take their own lives.

Throughout telling the story about the suicides, Dad had that strange smile on his face as if he knew a secret he didn't want to share. Then again, I might have been wrong.

Dad is a dyed in the wool rubbernecker. Lacking empathy for those in danger, he enjoys watching a good fire or disaster. Little did he realise that very soon, he'd be part of a personal disaster, and he wouldn't enjoy the experience one little bit.

"Why are you grinning?" Mary repeated. *"The ship's hit a mine!"*

"Carl Whyler's going to let *me* have a look at the mine damage from the main observation deck," Dad announced. "Apparently, one of the food production pods took the blast. As I said, though, was no one was hurt."

"What's a mine?" I asked.

"You'd better explain," Mary cut in, "In case you've forgotten, they didn't teach Earth history at Bee Bee's school."

When Dad's rugged face contorted with anger, I could tell that Mary's comment had ignited the blue touchpaper, "That's because Mars now has a namby-pamby government. They banned history lessons because Earth's history is full of wars. They also banned many other things, including my guns."

As Dad's rant continued, I vaguely recalled seeing the firearms he'd bought from Earth. Although they represented everything that the Mars authorities hated, Dad loved his guns; to him, they symbolised virility. They shouted death.

I also remembered watching him strip down his guns and clean them. While he was doing it, he winked at me and said, "A gun is like a woman Bee Bee; it has to be stripped down and serviced regularly."

I think the risqué joke was Dad's idea of father/son bonding.

It was during the gun cleaning that he told me that before he'd managed to get us evacuated to Mars, he was in the free corps, a local militia. Unless it was bragging, during that time, he'd killed a large number of people in shootouts. According to Dad, it was kill-or-be-killed in those days. Killing had become second nature.

I'd asked him how many people he'd killed. Dad just shrugged and said, "I lost count. Once you've killed, killing becomes very easy."

I said, "So you don't know how many people you've killed?"

Dad shrugged again, "We used mortars and grenade launchers against our enemies. Mortars and grenades kill more people than guns. Sometimes you don't see who you've killed."

It was then that Dad revealed his dark secret and why we were no longer using our real names. My father was a wanted man, a war criminal, and if it hadn't been for an underground movement who'd helped us escape, he would have been serving life imprisonment or given a death sentence.

Although the revelation shocked me, somehow, it didn't matter. He was still my Dad.

I also recalled how annoyed Dad had become when the **gun** amnesty started shortly after we'd arrived on Mars. There had been a general election, and the MPP swept to power. Being the dominant party, they swiftly pushed through their anti-war mandate even though it was controversial.

The Act didn't just cover firearms. Earth history books, violent video games, war-themed movies, and books involving gunplay or war themes also had to be handed in at police stations, government offices, or local libraries to be destroyed.

Eventually, Dad calmed down and, I repeated, "What's a mine, Dad?"

"They should have taught this at your school," Dad quibbled.

"Well, I can't help it," I said, "They didn't teach me about mines."

Relenting, Dad explained, "In simple form, a mine can just be a large explosive charge, but most modern mines are droids and are designed to home in on, and cause damage to, any passing space vehicle that doesn't supply it with the correct deactivation codes."

Sensing another question on the way, Dad added, "Before you ask, no one knows where the mine came from, Bee Bee. However, Carl Whyler said it confirms that humankind isn't alone in the universe."

"You mean it was an alien mine!"

"Carl Whyler told me that the fragments recovered from the outer shell of the mine had an unknown script on it," Dad confirmed. "Even computer analysis couldn't decipher it."

I was alarmed, "An alien mine! What happens if we hit another mine?"

My father was dismissive, "Carl Whyler said another strike was highly improbable because the ship has now erected a triple force shield defence. More importantly, the damage caused by the mine was only minor and will be repaired shortly."

Mary picked up on something that Dad had said earlier, "You said Carl Whyler would let *you* have a look at the mine damage. Don't *we* get a look in?"

"I didn't think you'd be interested," Dad replied defensively.

"I'm not," Mary replied. "But what about Bee Bee? If you take him, he can see how dangerous mines really are."

Dad glanced at me, "*Well*? D'you *want* to come too?"

The tone of his voice told me I wasn't welcome, and he seemed pleased when I shook my head. But just as I thought the matter settled, Mary said, "Go with your Dad, Bee Bee. I've no doubt it will fill in a few gaps in your education."

Dad's jaw muscles hardened with annoyance, but then, his demeanour changed, "Yeah. Why not Bee Bee. Like Mary says, seeing the damage will be educational."

Then, Dad became even more upbeat, "Another piece of news."

Holding up a card, he said, "Tomorrow, we've been invited to dine at the captain's table."

Mary's face fell, "I suppose Suzanna Fyfield will be there too."

Dad's anger flared up again, "I've told you before, nothing is going on between Suzanna Fyfield and me."

Mary just said, "I didn't say there was."

"No, you didn't," Dad snapped, "You didn't have to, but that was the implication."

There was a long pause, and I could tell that Mary didn't want to join Dad at the captain's table. But instead of objecting, Mary said, "That's very nice, Rob. I suppose we'll have to dress up."

"Of course," Dad said. "The captain's table means best bib and tucker. And put your falsies on too. Suspension doesn't do you any favours. You've gone as flat as a pancake as usual."

My face fell too; I liked to slob: jeans and a tee-shirt for me. I hated wearing smart clothes and pretending to have good table manners.

Chapter Two

Viewing the Damage

Five hours later, Dad began waving at a small view panel on one of the doors. Waiting inside, there was a man and a woman. Once the door opened, Dad introduced Carl Whyler and Suzanna Fyfield, Mary's supposed love rival.

As we stepped into the observation area, I heard Suzanna Fyfield whisper, "What did you bring him for?"

Dad whispered, "I didn't think you'd be here."

He glanced at me and raised his voice, "You wanted to come, didn't you, Bee Bee?"

Suzanna Fyfield glanced at me and then swiftly glanced away again. But I knew why. In a celebrity-driven culture, in the beautiful world, the uglies are shunned. After all, with plastic surgeons able to work miracles, did anyone have the right to be ugly?

Moving away from me, Suzanna said, "This area is restricted, so don't go shouting your mouth off when you leave. You're not really supposed to be in here."

"Understood," Dad replied.

He nudged me, and I added, "Understood."

Suzanna winked at Dad, "Don't forget Carl."

Dad reacted by slipping Whyler a small envelope, and I realised that my father was greasing palms to see the damage. As I followed Dad into the observation area, I ran an eye over Suzanna Fyfield and guessed she was about the same age as Mary, but there were marked differences.

Mary was short, skinny and plain; Suzanna was tall, had natural blonde hair, green eyes and went in and out in all the right places; I could understand why Mary felt threatened; Suzanna *was* stunning.

Noting I'd been left behind, Carl Whyler waved me in, "Come in, Bee Bee and take a look at the damage."

Stepping forward, I glanced out. Both Dad and I let out a simultaneous gasp as we looked at the remains of one of the food production pods. Dad, then, vocalised my thoughts, "You said there was only slight damage to the ship."

Carl Whyler said, "It's not as bad as it looks, Rob. The main structure, the rib cage, if you like, is still intact. The outer skin is reinforced plastimetal, and they will inflate a new bubble shortly. We should have the pod back in action within a week, and new fast-growing crops will be ready for harvest in four or five standard weeks."

Despite my father's previous assertions, I said, "What if the ship is hit by another mine? Or several even?"

"That's unlikely to happen, Bee Bee," Carl Whyler assured me, patting me on the shoulder, "The captain has turned on a triple shield. So stop worrying."

As we emerged from the main observation deck, Carl Whyler's face fell because someone was standing outside the observation room, and his demeanour suggested latent aggression.

After a slight pause, Suzanna Fyfield stepped forward and said, "Is there something wrong, Ed?"

Although I had never met Ed Fyfield before, I knew who he was because Dad had mentioned his name and had described his height, size, passion for bodybuilding and, like Dad, a love of guns. More importantly, the thin woven plastimetal uniform Ed Fyfield was wearing left an observer with little doubt about the muscle structure below.

Suzanna Fyfield repeated, "Is there something wrong, Ed?"

Instead of answering Suzanna's question, Ed Fyfield moved towards Carl Whyler and held out one massive hand, palm upwards. He said, "Give!"

Without arguing, Carl Whyler handed over the envelope Dad had slipped him. After dropping the payment into his pocket, Ed Fyfield growled, "I thought my instructions were clear. No one goes in there."

Carl Whyler submitted, "I won't take anyone else in there, sir. Suzanna said it was okay on this occasion."

Ed Fyfield glared at Suzanna, "I said, no one. And that includes boyfriends. No one goes in there until all the repairs have been made. Understood!"

Carl Whyler answered for her, "Understood, sir."

Fyfield then turned his attention to Dad and poked him in the chest with one of his massive fingers. He said, "Just because you're my sister's friend, it doesn't mean you can take liberties. Understood?"

Dad copied Carl Whyler's example and began churning out apologies. Instead of accepting them, Ed Fyfield glanced at me. After studying my face, Ed Fyfield ran a finger down one of my scars, half-smiled and said, "If you'd been a German army officer in the nineteenth or early twentieth century, that scar would have earned respect. It looks just like a duelling scar."

As I had no idea what he was talking about, I kept quiet. Eventually, Ed Fyfield added, "I presume you're Bee Bee."

When I nodded, Ed Fyfield said, "Well, Bee Bee, your Dad should be setting you a better example."

Ed Fyfield glared at Dad again, "He shouldn't be going where he shouldn't and chasing after every woman he meets."

Dad gulped; Suzanna flared, "What does that mean, Ed?"

Ed Fyfield eyed them both disdainfully and said, "Don't play the innocent with me. You know exactly what I mean. Playing suspension bed-hop. Did you really think it would go unnoticed?"

Once Ed Fyfield had given everyone another lambasting, his attitude suddenly changed. Glancing at Dad, he said, "Are you going to join us at the shooting range later on?"

Realising that Ed Fyfield was offering him an olive branch, Dad nodded, "That would be great, Ed."

Ed Fyfield glanced at me, "Have you ever shot a gun before?"

When I shook my head, Ed Fyfield said, "Time to learn. Bring him and Mary along."

I could immediately sense that Dad didn't want me there cramping his style, but Ed Fyfield gave him a sharp look and said, "We need to get your documents sorted out."

The expression on Dad's face suddenly changed, "Ah! Right. The documents."

As Ed Fyfield finally walked away, Dad gave me a nudge, tapped the side of his nose and said, "Don't say anything to Mary about this, okay!"

When I remained silent, Dad became more aggressive, "*Okay*?"

I was tempted to ask for clarification. Did Dad mean about being told off for going into a restricted area, bribing Carl Whyler, or was he asking me to stay schtum about his alleged relationship with Suzanna Fyfield?

When I didn't reply, Suzanna overcame her apparent dislike for my scars and went on a charm offensive. She gave me a winning smile, "I'm sure your Dad doesn't want to worry your stepmother about any of this. Despite what my brother implied, your dad and I are just friends. You won't say anything, will you, Bee Bee?"

Falling under Suzanna's spell, I nodded, "Okay. I won't say anything."

"Promise."

"Yeah!"

Dad cracked a smile and patted me on one shoulder, "Thanks, Bee Bee. I appreciate it."

But once we'd left Carl Whyler and Suzanna Fyfield and began walking back to our apartment, Dad became more forceful, "You don't say anything to Mary when we get back, right! If you do. I'll make you regret it."

"I said I wouldn't."

"Well, don't!"

Although I kept my promise, I felt very guilty. Deep down, I knew Dad was lying, and I didn't want to be disloyal to Mary.

~*~

A few hours later, Dad took Mary and me to the recreation area, and I was amazed at how crowded it was. As some people were wearing ships colours, I guessed they were crew. The rest were passengers.

Seeing us, Ed Fyfield unwound himself from an exercise machine, came to greet us and said, "Glad you could make it."

I expected him to take us straight to the shooting range, but instead, he led us to a side office. Glancing at Dad, Ed Fyfield opened one hand. It was the same action he'd used when confiscating Carl Whyler's bribe.

Dad responded by handing over a large envelope. Ed Fyfield retreated behind a cabinet. As I could hear money being counted, I guessed that Dad had just handed over the last payment for our new identities.

I heard a safe being opened, the money swapping for documents, and Ed Fyfield returned. However, before handing over our new IDs, Ed Fyfield told Dad to give him the forged documents that allowed us to board the Empress of Incognita.

Once he was satisfied, he then presented us with our official IDs.

When Dad started inspecting what he'd been given, Ed Fyfield said, "Don't worry. They'll pass muster, and once the ship reaches the Kepler-452 system, I will make sure that you and your family are well looked after. It's all part of the service."

When Dad nodded, Ed Fyfield then said, "Right! That's that complete; I'll take you down to the shooting range."

Once there, Dad introduced me to a rifle, showed me how to use it and then let me pump away at a target in a well-padded enclosure. Once I'd finished, Dad began instructing Mary on the art of gunmanship.

I sat down, but I wasn't on my own for long because Chas Foony saw me, gave me a wave and came over. I was pleased to see him because there were very few people of my age on the Empress of Incognita, or if there were, they must have been in different suspension groups.

After slumping down beside me, Chas said, "So what are you doing here?"

"Ed Fyfield invited us," Chas replied. "And you?"

"The same," Chas said.

He let out a slight laugh, "I think he uses the same invitation for everyone when he has documents to hand out to rat liners."

"Rat liners?"

Chas shook his head, "You're very naive, you know that, Bee Bee. Or maybe it was the bang on the head that made you that way."

The comment annoyed me slightly, and I half regretted telling Chas about the car crash. Referring to my accident as a bang on the head was flippant in the extreme, but I let it pass. Instead, I said, "Go on. Educate me, Chas. What's a rat liner?"

"The Earth security authorities unofficially refer to the likes of my parents and your Dad as rats," Chas replied, "The escape routes used by rats are ratlines."

"Why do they call them rats?"

Chas shrugged, "Not many people like war criminals. Anyway, that's the unofficial name that Earth authorities use to describe people being hunted for war crimes. Other than us, I would guess that practically everyone on this ship would probably come under that classification."

"Not everyone, surely," I replied. "What about Mary?"

As usual, Chas was dispassionate, "Your mother died. I heard my parents talking about it. My guess is your father needed a woman to take with him. Kepler-452 only takes approved couples and family members."

"So you're saying that Dad is just with Mary so he can escape justice!"

"Correct!"

I felt so annoyed I nearly punched Chas, but he grabbed my fist and then nodded in Mary and Dad's direction and said, "Look at the body language. She obviously loves him, but he's just pretending."

"That's not true," I snapped defensively, even though I knew he might be right.

"Then why is your Dad sniffing around Suzanna Fyfield?

"He's not!"

"He is," Chas insisted.

Because I didn't want to think about the possibility that Dad had grown bored with Mary, I deliberately changed the subject back to the original discussion, "Surely, the ship's crew can't *all* be wanted."

Chas said, "On the contrary, ships like the Empress provide perfect bolt holes for some criminals. Finding starship crews isn't easy."

"Why?"

Chas shrugged, "It just isn't."

"That's not an answer," I replied.

Chas said, "Star travel might seem fantastic in the movies. However, when people realise that there is probably no return ticket, they change their minds."

"No return ticket?"

"People start to age differently on a starship," Chas replied. "I don't understand why, but if you go on a long journey and then return to Earth, no one you once knew is alive. So there is no point coming back. Even if you did, you wouldn't be able to make yourself understood."

"Why not?"

"Because language evolves," Chas replied. "People who lived five hundred years ago would not be able to talk to us easily, methinks."

"Eh!"

Chas grinned, "It was a joke. Methinks—that's how they used to talk in the olden days, get it?"

"Yeah," I replied. "Very funny."

Chas added, "That's why many recruitment agencies don't ask too many questions and offer free training and high wages to obtain suitable crew. They are so desperate to fill positions they take most volunteers."

Chas nodded towards Ed Fyfield, "He's a typical example. My father met him during the uprising."

"And?"

"Everyone was scared of him," Chas replied. "In those days, he carried a large knife, more like a sword, and used it to kill prisoners. He beheaded some if he felt like it. Even his own forces feared him; they called him *The Butcher*. Of course, he was given a new ID to work on the Empress of Incognita, but it doesn't alter the fact that he killed hundreds of people and used prisoners as slave labour. He's a total psychopath."

Chas jabbed me in the arm, "I told you that in confidence. So don't go shouting about it. I don't want Ed Fyfield coming after me."

When my parents finished at the firing range, Chas stood up and said, "I'll give you a call tomorrow if you're free."

"That would be great," I said.

Although I wasn't sure if everything that Chas had told me was true, it made me think. Maybe I overthought it.

~*~

Once I'd gone to bed, I had the same dream I'd had when I came out of suspension. Within seconds of going to sleep, I found myself back in the dark pyramid with the bright light at the top. As per usual, the bony arms and hands reached out. Then my mother's face appeared, and her lips started moving, but I still couldn't hear her.

I started to fall, and just before I hit the bottom of the cavern, my father's laughing face appeared again.

My dream suddenly changed when a face I didn't know popped up in my mind and said, "You are in great danger, Bee Bee. Choose your friends carefully."

My mind re-ran the entire pyramid dream again and ended with my Dad's laughing face.

Suddenly, I was awake, and Dad was standing over me, but he wasn't laughing. He said, "You've been having those dreams again, haven't you, Bee Bee?"

"Those dreams?" I replied.

"The ones you keep writing about in your diary," Dad replied.

I felt angry. Very angry. Dad had openly admitted that he'd been snooping in my private diary. Seeing the expression on my face, Dad was unapologetic, "I only looked because I'm worried about you."

"Why?"

"Because it's obvious you are very troubled," Dad replied. "Maybe you need...."

Knowing where the conversation was going, I cut in, "I don't need to see a psycho-quack if that is what you are driving at."

"After the accident, you were very ill...."

"I'm fine now," I insisted.

"You were screaming out for your mother. You've done that before," Dad replied.

"I'm okay," I replied. "I've just had a few bad dreams."

"Okay," Dad said, "Let's leave it there. Now get some sleep."

Once he'd left my room, I became anxious. Why did I keep seeing my mother, and what was she trying to tell me? And why did my dream always end with Dad laughing at me?

And where had the strange person come from? The one who'd said, "You are in great danger, Bee Bee. Choose your friends carefully."

I began thinking about what Chas had told me. On the one hand, I wanted to believe that Dad was playing fair by Mary, yet I was virtually positive he was lying.

Chapter Three

More Mine Strikes

The following day, I was kicking my heels. Although I like Mary, I felt like a spare wheel cramped up in the apartment.

Besides, being party to Dad's secrets made me uncomfortable. Was Dad lying, or was his relationship with Suzanna Fyfield purely platonic? Should I go back on my promises and snitch him up to Mary if Dad was lying?

I thought of the consequences. If I discovered Dad was lying and betrayed him, he'd probably disown me. I needed time to think.

Luckily, my mobile phone rang, and Chas Foony's avatar popped up next to a text and suggested another hangout.

Dad had fallen asleep in a chair, so I glanced at Mary, "I'm going down to rotunda five."

I expected resistance, but Mary just said, "Okay, but don't get into trouble. And don't be too late back for your evening meal."

I grimaced and turned sarcastic, "An Empress special – I can't wait."

Five seconds later, I was out of the door and making my way to rotunda five. When I arrived, Chas was staring at one of the shop windows surrounding the circular dome. I said, "So what are you after?"

Chas blew a raspberry, "At these prices—nothing!"

I had to agree. The Empress of Incognita operated a captive audience policy, and the prices of most goods were extortionate. The same applied to meals served up by the autochef in our apartment. Although the basic menu, the *Empress specials* as we called them, were included in the transportation fee, anything tasting like real food came at a steep premium.

After mooching over to a seating area, Chas waved a bottle he was carrying and said, "Wanna drink?"

I recalled the last time he'd offered me a drink, "Is it demon brew?"

Chas grinned and then nodded, "Want some?"

When I nodded back, he produced two grubby plastic beakers and poured out the fizzy liquid. I took a sip; it didn't taste too bad, "Did you make this?"

Chas shook his head, "Nar, my Dad makes it."

Nodding towards the shops, Chas added, "He won't pay *their* prices for drinks."

I was tempted to ask what it was made from, but Chas caught my tongue when he asked, "So what do you make of this mine strike?"

"My Dad said the mine strike was hush-hush."

Chas laughed, "Someone heard the crew gossiping. Things like a mine strike don't remain secret for long."

I was tempted to admit that I had no idea what a mine was until Dad explained, but I played along, not wishing to seem stupid.

While we were still discussing the strike, Chas said, "Apparently, most starships avoid the wormhole we're in because other ships have suffered damage here in the past. There was talk of sweeping the wormhole, but it would cost billions."

I must have looked shocked because Chas added, "My Dad reckons the captain took the risk of going down this wormhole to save fuel and money."

"You're joking!"

Chas shook his head, "I've heard this wormhole cuts three months off the flight time. Other ships have used the route and have got through unscathed. I guess the captain got unlucky."

He added, "I hope we don't get really unlucky."

"What do you mean?"

Chas shrugged, "Most mines are laid in swarms. If we've hit one, there could be others homing in on us even as we speak."

My fears emerged again, "D'you think we *will* hit another mine? What about the force shield?"

Chas shrugged again, "I was talking to someone else about that. Apparently, triple force shields can be very effective, but some sophisticated mines can create windows in the force shields and get through."

Later, I realised that Chas was right.

~*~

When we arrived at the Captain's entertainment suite, Suzanna Fyfield was there. She gave Dad and Mary a beaming smile, but she didn't look at me; I presumed that now she'd extracted a vow of silence from me, I was back to being an ugly untouchable.

Dining with Captain Wainwright went very well until I forgot that I was privy to hush-hush information and said, "Have *you* ever seen the aliens, Captain?"

Wainwright gave me a penetrating stare, "What aliens?"

Suzanna Fyfield also gave me an icy look, and I felt Dad kick me under the table, but it didn't stop me from blurting out, "The aliens that made the mine that damaged the Empress of Incognita."

Captain Wainwright's irises shrunk to the size of pinheads, "How did you find out about the mine?"

Realising that Suzanna Fyfield and Carl Whyler might get into trouble, I thought fast. Recalling my conversation with Chas, I said, "I thought everyone knew: one of my mates told me about it."

"What mate?"

"His name is Chas."

"Chas what? What's his last name?"

I shrugged and lied, "I just call him Chas. I don't know what his other name is. We just hang out sometimes."

Wainwright gave me another icy look, "Well, tell this Chas friend of yours not to go around creating panic. For your information, the explosion caused very little damage."

I was tempted to ask why we were using a dangerous wormhole but didn't because another kick in the shins warned me off.

Without prompting, Wainwright added, "The wormhole we're using does appear to contain mines, but the ship's computer system has been placed on high alert, so it is unlikely we will hit any more mines. If mines close in on us, the force shields will make them explode before they can cause us any damage."

I was about to query Wainwright's assurances, but another kick in the shin changed my mind. After that, the conversation became very strained, and as a result, we finally thanked our host and left.

Once back in our apartment, Dad chastised me, "Why did you raise the issue of mines and aliens with the captain?"

"I thought everyone knew about the mine."

"Well, they didn't!"

I was still being told off when the ship shuddered underfoot, and it jerked twice more in swift succession. Then, a moment later, the alarms went off, and a computer-generated voice began saying, "Please vacate your apartment and go to your designated assembly point in rotunda five."

Then there was hammering on the outer door. When Dad opened it, Carl Whyler stood there and said, "This is not a drill. Make your way calmly to your assembly point in rotunda five. I said calmly; don't run."

Whyler then moved off, hammering on other doors and giving out the same message. Despite the Captain's assurances, I realised that other mines had hit the Empress of Incognita. As the starship had shuddered, logic dictated that the other mines must have been far larger than the first one.

When we arrived at rotunda five, Chas Foony was there, but he was alone, so I went over to him. Eventually, I asked the obvious question, "Where are your Mum and Dad?"

Chas pointed towards one section of the dome where the bulkhead doors had dropped and said, "My parents fight a lot, so I came here to get away from the arguments. I'd only been here a few minutes when the whole ship shook and the emergency shutters dropped. I checked the shutter; there's ice forming on our side. "

I gulped. The implications of what Chas had just said meant that the zone beyond the shutter had depressurised, and the intense cold of outer space would have claimed the area.

I vaguely recall making the sort of pointless expressions of sorrow that people make in such situations. Once I'd finished, Chas shrugged and said, "I don't suppose they suffered."

I was surprised by the callousness in the comment but began thinking about Chas's dysfunctional family life. From what Chas had told me, his parents had spent most of their waking hours at each other's throats; Chas had lost his parents long before they'd actually died.

My thoughts swept me back to my childhood in Mars Base 5, and I thought about the Void Monster for the first time in months.

Without a doubt, the Void Monster had killed Chas Foony's family.

Perhaps I'd better explain. Although I'd always know that the Void Monster didn't really exist, the spikey Jack Frost image had always stuck in my mind. The VM was part of a Mars government safety drive designed to dissuade children from opening an airlock and going outside without wearing a pressure suit. The advertisements implied that the void monster would kill them stone dead if they did.

After giving Chas my deepest sympathies, I took him back to my parents and explained the situation as he was on his own.

Once they'd given him *their* condolences, they glanced towards the bulkhead doors and went white; they'd realised that the ice-covered emergency shutter was the only thing keeping them alive. Death wasn't far away.

My parent's display of nerves visibly increased when the shop droids left their posts and came out into the rotunda. The tension rose even higher as the shutters descended in front of each shop.

The shop droids moved around the crowded rotunda, taking names, apartment numbers and the names of missing persons. Once that task was complete, they opened up a shutter to an emergency exit tunnel and began herding us down it.

Halfway down the tunnel, the alarms sounded again, and then a heavy shutter crashed home, preventing anyone from returning to Rotunda five.

I felt the ship shudder underfoot again, the lights went out, and everyone started screaming.

The droids responded by turning on their body lights. A few seconds later, the emergency lighting cut in. Then, another shudder later, the emergency lights flickered off and flickered on again.

After walking for some distance, the emergency tunnel widened into an area containing a solitary airlock and a medium-sized shuttlecraft. More heavy shutters began dropping behind us once we were well inside the shuttlecraft zone.

Glancing around the area, I realised that there were no apparent means of escape other than the shuttle, not even a solitary life pod.

At that point, my Dad's devil may care attitude to life completely evaporated, and he said, "This looks bad, Mary."

Carl Whyler suddenly appeared, and Dad grabbed hold of one of his arms and said, "What's going on, Carl?"

"I'm just about to make an announcement," Whyler replied and shook himself free. He moved into the group's centre and used an amplification system on one of the droids to make himself heard. After explaining that the passengers had only been sent to the shuttle bay as a safety precaution, he pointed towards the fixed seating, "Please, make yourselves comfortable; food and drink will be brought shortly."

Five minutes later, more droids appeared and began distributing food and drinks. Dad tried to engage Carl

Whyler in conversation again, but he followed one of the droids into a staff-only area and disappeared.

Ignoring the staff-only sign, Dad went after him. Twenty minutes later, Dad returned, and his face was the whitest I'd ever seen it.

"What did he say, Dad? Is it bad?"

"Keep your voice down, Bee Bee!" he snapped. He then lowered his voice, "Sorry, we don't want to start a panic now, do we?"

He moved toward Mary. Not wishing to miss anything, Chas and I moved in close and heard him whisper, "I thought it was bad, and it is. It would appear that the captain and several senior officers have been killed."

Dad added, "I think Ed and Suzanna Fyfield may have died too."

Mary gave him a strange look that half implied sympathy but also suggested relief; her love rival was dead. As I suspected that Dad had been carrying on an affair with Suzanna Fyfield, I could understand her feelings.

Although lacking in empathy, from my point of view, Suzanna Fyfield's reported death made me feel a lot better too. If Suzanna Fyfield *had* died during the mine attack, she'd become history, and I didn't need to say anything to Mary.

While I was still thinking, Chas said, "If the captain and senior officers are dead, who's in charge?"

Dad shrugged, "In here, Carl Whyler. As far as I can tell, the rest of the ship is controlled by the ship's auxiliary computer. The main computer is kaput."

"Is that it?" Mary whispered back. "Is that all the news?"

"No," Dad replied. "Not exactly. As far as Carl Whyler can tell, the auxiliary computer is following an emergency program."

When Mary and I remained silent, Dad added, "Carl also told me that the ship has suffered a great deal of damage; it's been hit by another five mines."

"Five mines!"

Dad nodded, "Six if you count the first one. Apparently, the ship is trying to escape further mine attacks and has diverted course into a minor wormhole branch."

I frowned. Although my schooling had been poor, curtailed and corrupted by anti-war sentiments, I did know the basics of star travel. Every diagram I'd seen of a wormhole structure indicated it only had two open ends, so I said, "I didn't know that wormholes could branch."

Dad shrugged again. He looked drained, "To be honest, most of what Carl Whyler told me went over my head. If I understood correctly, the ship has entered an unexplored branch wormhole."

"Unexplored?"

"That's what he said," Dad replied, "Apparently, there are hundreds of small wormholes all over the place. As exploration and evaluation funding is in short supply, large numbers are still unknown territory."

While we were still talking about what the future might hold for us, the noise levels in the escape bay suddenly increased. Recognising faces from the apartment register, Dad said, "That's the Whistons; they must have been brought out of suspension."

Mary immediately pulled a face, "Well, whatever you do, don't go over and talk to them because it will only spark an argument. We've got enough trouble without starting a fight with that load of scumbags."

Although Dad did as instructed, he still let his gaze wander towards the untidy timeshare family who'd blighted our lives. As I continued to stare in the Whiston's direction, Chas's previous comments echoed in my mind. If what he'd told me was correct, the chances were the Whistons were also criminals on the run, unemotional killers who dispatched their fellow humans without it troubling their consciences.

While we were still watching, one of the Whistons started an argument with another family and forced them off the benches they were sitting on. I half expected other people to intervene, but no one did. Even the droids ignored the incident.

The next thing I knew, Chas Foony walked over and began talking to the man who'd forced the family off the benches. I later discovered that his name was Dugal Whiston.

Whiston immediately squared up to Chas. As Dugal Whiston was tall, broad-shouldered and had the build of a heavyweight boxer, I expected to see Chas flattened, but the exact opposite happened.

Whiston lunged, and the next moment he went flying through the air and landed unceremoniously on his back, gasping like a beached whale.

When Whiston just lay there winded, Chas ordered the Whiston family to move and waved the other family back to their seats.

One or two people clapped, but the majority stayed silent. They didn't want to get involved.

Once Chas had returned, I said. "How did you pull that off?"

"My Dad gave me self-defence training," Chas replied. "But now I'll have to watch my back."

"Why?"

"Because people like Dugal Whiston bear grudges," Chas replied. "He'll want to get back at me, for sure."

He added, "It's a pity Ed Fyfield isn't here."

"Why?"

"Because Dugal Whiston tried it on with Ed Fyfield a few weeks ago. He objected to going back into suspension. He was demanding to be allowed to have special treatment, a permanent apartment of his own. A fight broke out, and Fyfield flattened him," Chas replied.

Chas laughed.

"What's so funny?"

"When Dugal Whiston complained to the ship's authorities claiming that Fyfield had started the fight, Fyfield was exonerated."

"How come?"

"It was recorded on CCTV. Ed Fyfield was just defending himself," Chas replied. "Whiston threw the first punch."

"Yeah, your right. It's a pity Ed Fyfield isn't here," I agreed.

Although I didn't like Ed Fyfield one bit, having someone around who could tackle the likes of Whiston would have been helpful.

Chapter Four

Entering the Salus System

We spent the best part of three weeks in the shuttle bay. By the end of that period, the air was fetid because the air purification system wasn't working properly, and the droids had started rationing food to ensure it didn't run out. The lighting was also reduced to save power.

To keep fit, some people ran up and down the accessible areas, but the practice was swiftly abandoned because, in the cramped environment, the runners and joggers were annoying too many people. They were also helping to exhaust precious oxygen.

When the lighting was turned off to simulate night, some people slept on the benches, and others slept on the floor.

Although most people felt they were in limbo land, we were given bulletins from time to time because Carl Whyler made announcements. Eventually, we were told that the Empress of Incognita was heading towards an unknown semi-Earth type planet; Someone dubbed it Arcadia, and the name stuck.

~*~

When the Empress of Incognita finally went into orbit around Arcadia, there was a rush towards the blister windows, but the surface looked disappointing. Although oceans of water were visible, most landmasses appeared to be desert. Then, as the planet slowly turned, a vast island continent came into view, and it was swiftly named New Australia.

More importantly, several parts of New Australia were covered in what looked like green vegetation.

While we were still staring out, Chas moved alongside me and said, "I'm going to make myself scarce, and if I were you, I'd do so too."

"Why?"

"Because I think that Dugal Whiston has got a gun," Chas said. "I think he's also armed some of his friends."

"Where did they get the guns?"

"From the lockers in the gun club," Chas replied. "My guess he's ripped open one of the lockers and has taken the guns and ammunition."

"How d'you know?"

"I don't know for certain," Chas admitted, "but I've heard people talking, and Whiston has what looks like a rifle bag propped up next to him."

"If you think he's got a gun and other people have guns, shouldn't we tell someone?"

Chas said, "I've already done that, but Carl Whyler has already had several run-ins with Whiston and is scared of him. More importantly, Whyler is not part of the ship's police force, so he's keeping his distance from Whiston. He doesn't want to get shot either."

I said, "But where are the ship's police?"

"I guess they're trapped in an area similar to this one," Chas replied, "That is if any of them are still alive, of course. As the ship has been hit at least six times, they could be dead for all we know."

Chas then added, "I think Dugal Whiston will come looking for me."

"Surely not."

"That's what I've heard people saying," Chas replied. He added, "He's not made any secret about getting even. He's seen you with me, so he might decide to shoot your family too."

"He wouldn't dare; that's murder."

Chas shook his head in disbelief, "What world are you living in? People get murdered every day. There are no police around, and Whiston is a violent and vindictive man."

Giving up hope of the ship's authorities intervening, I said, "But where can we hide?"

"I've found a place," Chas replied.

He nodded towards Dad and Mary, my parents, "I'd get them out of harm's way too if I were you. Don't forget, Dugal Whiston has a beef with them too; they reported him for leaving a mess in your apartment. Tell them to bring all the food and water they have."

Taking Chas's advice, I had a quick word with my parents and was amazed when they followed, but then from the things they said on the way, it was apparent they'd heard the whispers too. Whiston intended to take the law into his own hands, knowing that it was unlikely there would be any repercussions.

By the time that we arrived, Chas had removed a ventilation grill. Waving at the opening, he said, "Get in."

Once I'd stooped to get in, I found myself in a large ventilation duct. After my parents had piled in, Chas refixed the grill and applied fast-acting glue to the fittings.

I was tempted to ask him where he'd found the glue, but I let the issue slide as it didn't seem important.

Once Chas had finished gluing, he led the way down the duct and didn't stop walking until we headed down a large side branch.

Hearing him let out a sigh of relief, I asked, "Why have you come so far in?"

"Because Dugal Whiston will probably work out we're in the duct and might start firing in the hope of hitting us," Chas replied. He tapped part of the duct directly behind where we were standing. "This section runs directly behind a bulkhead wall, and it should be bulletproof."

"How d'you know there's a bulkhead?"

Chas pointed at a large security sign confirming what he'd just told me. He then added, "I've been down here before, exploring. On a ship this size, they have to make sure some idiot doesn't damage a bulkhead by mistake."

"So, what do we do now?"

"We wait," Chas said.

"Wait for what?"

"For Dugal Whiston to make his move," Chas replied. "I've heard whispers that he intends to hijack the shuttle.

Presumably, Dugal Whiston wants to make sure his people escape, and the rest of us can go hang."

Chas added, "Its Catch 22. If we leave this duct, Whiston will kill us for sure, and if we don't, the shuttle goes without us.

My Dad cut in, "Not exactly Catch 22. If we stay here, there is a strong possibility that someone will rescue us once Whiston's mob have left."

Chapter Five

A Giant Arcadian Millipede Gets Aboard the Empress

Dugal Whiston made his move about two hours after we went into hiding. As we'd kept as quiet as we could, I heard Whiston shout out, "Are you sure they came this way?"

His lackey called back, "Sure, I'm sure. You told me to keep an eye on them, so I did. They came down here."

The grill we'd climbed through rattled, and Whiston's voice said, "They're probably hiding in the ductwork."

The grill rattled again. Eventually, Whiston snapped, "It's jammed, so they can't have gone in there."

Whiston shouted, "Get Carl Whyler down here."

A few minutes later, I heard Whiston snap, "Can you get this grill off?"

The grill rattled again, and Whyler said, "Sorry. It's stuck."

We heard a loud noise and realised that Whiston was shooting at the grill.

Whyler's voice cut in, "Stop, stop. No shooting! You could puncture the hull."

After a short pause, I heard Whiston say, "Okay, you win. No more shooting."

He laughed, "If Chas Foony and the Kinfrank family have hidden in the ducting and no one rescues them, they'll die a slow death anyway. Right, let's go. "

Whyler said, "Go where?"

"To the shuttle," Whiston replied.

"But you can't take the shuttle," Whyler protested.

"You've got a choice," Whiston replied. "You get us off the Empress of Incognita, or I'll start shooting people. What's it going to be?"

"I'm not a pilot," Whyler whined.

Whiston made tutting noises, "Don't try to bullshit me, Carl. You're a junior officer, and the ship's computer has gone into emergency response mode. The shuttle will obey your verbal commands and put us down safely on Arcadia."

"Where d'you want to put down?"

Although the conversation became muffled, the snippets I overheard suggested that Whiston wanted the shuttle to touch down in the valley near the high plateau in New Australia, in one of the green areas we'd observed.

When the talking stopped, I waited expectantly. Instead, we heard raised voices followed by gunfire. Moments later, there was the sound of running feet. My mind began painting a possible scenario; the panicking passengers had tried to prevent Whiston and his gang from stealing the shuttle, so Whiston had started shooting. As he was used to violence, it came easily.

Two minutes later, vague noises came vibrating through the ship's hull. Chas provided his interpretation,

"They've launched the shuttle, and they are going to Arcadia and leaving us behind."

"Meaning we're trapped in here unless someone tries to rescue us," Dad said.

Chas shook his head, "Not necessarily. I can release the grill."

"We're still trapped on the Empress, though," Dad snapped.

Chas shook his head again, "The shuttle will probably return."

"How d'you make that out?" Dad replied. "Judging by what Whiston said, he'll keep the shuttle and leave us to die."

"The Empress's computer system controls the shuttle," Chas replied. "Unless Whiston can prevent the shuttle from returning, I suspect that once it has landed and once Whiston's people have disembarked, the shuttle will return automatically."

Although I could tell that Dad was relieved by Chas's predictions, he still gave a slightly hostile response, "How come you're an expert?"

Chas grinned, "I wasn't brought up on Mars, so I watched lots of sci-fi movies."

~*~

After being locked in the duct for some time, we worked up the courage to remove the glue on the grill using a solvent that Chas had in his pocket and step out into the shuttle bay again.

We glanced around the corner, noticed that the shuttle was missing, and moved cautiously forward. A few steps later, the scene turned horrific. There were bodies strewn all over the place, and a droid was on fire.

Chas said, "Good job, we hid. That would have been us for sure."

After using an extinguisher on the droid to prevent the fire from spreading, Dad moved around the bodies, checking for signs of life. Failing to find survivors, he widened the search and eventually returned with several frightened people in tow.

Although it was apparent that Whiston and/or his gang had opened fire on the crowd, Mary asked, "Who did this?"

Every mouth spat out the same name, "Dugal Whiston."

~*~

The airlock activated just over six hours later, and the shuttle returned as Chas had predicted. Once the airlock had gone through its decontamination procedures, it refilled with air, and Carl Whyler emerged and raced towards the internal door, swiftly moved through it, slammed it hard behind him, and made sure it was locked.

The door bolts had barely hammered into position before a giant serpent-like creature hurled itself at the transparent door and began raking its teeth on it.

As the rasping teeth continued working on the door, plumes of smoke began drifting around the airlock.

Someone nearby screamed out, "It's using some sort of acid to burn its way through. It's trying to get in!"

Gripped by fear, the rubberneckers backed away. But Carl Whyler just stood there as if mesmerised by the alien creature.

For reasons best known to itself, the beast suddenly lost interest in the door and began moving around the airlock, and it stopped, half-climbed up a glazed wall exposing its multi-legged body and stared directly at me.

Feeling ill at ease, I moved, but as I did so, the beast moved with me, keeping its eyes firmly locked on me. Thinking it was just a coincidence, I moved again. The giant Arcadian millipede moved with me again and sent me a message that seemed to echo in my mind, "When I escape from here, you will be the first to die. The Great Ones have commanded it."

I had little doubt that the message was meant for me because the beast was still staring directly at me. The millipede went back to the door. But instead of raking its teeth on the door itself, it began attacking the door frame.

After the creature had been ripping off large chunks of the plastimetal lining for several minutes, Whyler let out a gasp of horror. Glancing at the doorway, I realised the giant millipede had pulled out some electrical cabling and was chewing on it.

Seconds later, there were several blinding flashes, and the lighting went off. But despite the darkness, the giant millipede was clearly visible because sparks were arcing down its body.

Eventually, the giant millipede broke free of the wiring with a twist of its body. But instead of attacking the door frame again, the creature began thrashing around, gripped by involuntary spasms. Its death throes continued for at least a minute, and then they stopped, but I could still see luminous smoke billowing from its body.

Once the emergency lights came on, Whyler cautiously moved towards the door and stared out. He let out a sigh of relief before announcing, "Thank God, I think it's electrocuted itself."

As the main lighting returned, we all moved closer to stare at the alien. As it was completely still, everyone agreed that it was well and truly dead; it had kicked the bucket for sure.

As my life had been threatened, I breathed a huge sigh of relief. Dead, the giant millipede couldn't carry out its threat. After staring at the beast for some time, I wondered who the Great Ones were and why they would want me to die.

In answer to my mental question, a voice whispered in my mind, "The Great Ones want to kill you because they see you as a threat."

I thought, "Who are the Great Ones, and how can I be a threat to them?"

In answer, the voice whispered, "You have skills that they fear. You must be careful."

I heard a distinct click in my mind as the voice cut off communication. No doubt I would have continued thinking about the Great Ones, but one of the women pointed at Whyler's left shoulder and let out a squeal of alarm, "You're bleeding."

She pointed at the flimsy bandage Whyler had tied around his injury. It had blood oozing through it.

Forgetting the defunct millipede, Mary and other women took Whyler into a washroom, and Chas, Dad and I followed.

Once he'd been cleaned up and bandaged, Dad began asking the obvious questions. Whyler said, "Whiston made me instruct the shuttle to land in a clearing by a large river. Once the doors were open, Whiston told some of the passengers to check out the area near the shuttle. As they walked through some the strange-looking grass like plants, they were ambushed by those giant millipede things."

Whyler added, "Whiston and his gang began firing at the millipedes, but there were hundreds of them; it was as if they knew where we were going to land and had assembled to attack us."

When Whyler let out a mournful sigh, Dad prompted him, "So what happened then?"

"Whiston closed the outer doors and told me to take off again," Whyler said. "He just abandoned everyone who was outside. But before we could take off, hundreds of the giant millipedes hurled themselves onto the shuttle and tried to stop us from leaving by weighing the shuttle down. Luckily, the engines worked overtime, and despite the extra weight, the shuttle took off again. Finally, after making the shuttle jink a few times, the millipedes dropped off."

Whyler added, "After that, Whiston told me to find a better place to land, so we left the clearing and landed on a large river island."

"You said that the millipedes dropped off," Dad said. "So, how come that one came up with you?"

Whyler shrugged, "It must have hidden somewhere. Probably in the landing gear."

Chas said, "Which meant it survived in space."

"It looks that way," Whyler replied. "I don't know how it managed to survive without breathing, though. Its armoured body segments must be as tough as hell."

Whyler then changed his mind, "Then again, it just died from electrocution. So maybe it wasn't so tough after all."

"So what happened to Whiston and his cronies?" Dad said.

"Once we'd landed on the river island," Whyler replied. "Whiston sent out some more people to check out the area, but they were reluctant to go in case more millipedes attacked. Whiston fired over their heads and forced them out at gunpoint."

"After half an hour, they returned and reported that they'd not run into any more millipedes," Whyler added. "So Whiston instructed them to unload the supplies. I recall telling Whiston he'd taken more supplies than he was entitled to."

Whyler then pointed to his bandaged shoulder, "Instead of discussing it with me, he just turned his rifle on me and shot me. I think he would have killed me in cold blood, but the shuttle reacted and expelled him."

Dad frowned, "How did it expel him?"

"With an internal force shield," Whyler replied.

"So what happened then?

Whyler shrugged, "I don't remember much after that; I must have passed out. I only came around when the shuttle started to dock. Then I caught a glimpse of the millipede, and I decided to make a run for it. The rest, you know."

Whyler added, "One good thing about being shot, Whiston didn't have a chance to unload most of the supplies."

Once Whyler had finished his tale, we all walked back to the airlock and pointed at the dead millipede, "As I said, the Empress's computer must have ordered the shuttle's return. I was lucky that the millipede didn't kill me."

Dad eyed the millipede thoughtfully, "Are you sure it's dead?"

"No," Whyler admitted. "That's why I'm going to send in a droid. Once it's taken tissue and poison samples, I want to see if we can get rid of it."

Chas echoed, "Poison samples?"

"I saw the millipedes spitting poison," Whyler said. "From what I saw, the venom is extremely virulent. Everyone hit by the venom died very quickly. I'd like to know what we're dealing with and find an antidote if we can."

Dad followed up with, "Why do you need tissue samples?"

"To make sure that Arcadia hasn't any other nasty surprises in store for us," Whyler replied.

I could see the obvious question forming on my father's lips, but he just said, "Once you've done your testing, then what?"

"While the analysis is being completed, we need to use the shuttle to check out the rest of the ship for survivors," Whyler replied

"Then what?"

"I suggest we leave while we still can and find somewhere safe on Arcadia's surface."

"Why can't we stay on the Empress?" Mary suggested.

Whyler shook his head, "Normally, I would suggest we stay with the ship and wait to be rescued. But rescue is highly improbable."

"Why?" Dad demanded.

"Because the ship was forced into an unexplored wormhole," Whyler replied. "So it's unlikely anyone will pick up our distress calls or know where to look for us."

Whyler sighed again, "You may as well know the truth. As the shuttle docked, I caught a glimpse of the Empress and saw how badly damaged the ship was. The only reason we are still alive is that the bulkheads have held, and if they fail, we're done for."

Mary said, "What about Whiston?"

Whyler shrugged again, "There is nothing that I can do about him, but we must try to find some weapons to take with us in case we run into him again."

After instructing a droid to enter the airlock, Whyler watched the machine drill through the millipedes' armoured segments and take samples of the creature's venom and body fluids at various locations. Once the droid had finished, it expelled the millipede's body into space via a personnel airlock.

After the droid had returned and decontaminated, Whyler took the samples for analysis. Dad and I followed.

As Whyler began giving instructions to the droid, Dad said, "What aren't you telling us? Why did you instruct the droid to take body fluids from that millipede?"

"You'll see," Whyler replied and watched the droid as it deposited the venom and body fluids into several analysers.

Within seconds red lights began flashing. As I'd followed Dad over, I said, "What's Carl doing?"

Overhearing me, Carl Whyler said, "During the panic to leave the ship, most of the groups ignored standard procedures."

Dad latched onto the comment, "What procedures?"

Whyler said, "The backup computer is still functioning. Its records suggest the evacuation became a mass panic in most areas. Although some crew members followed evacuation procedures, most passengers who used the life pods did so without crew guidance. Those records also indicate that, despite warnings, only a few probes went down, and very few samples were analysed before the evacuation started."

When Dad asked more questions, Whyler said, "That's why I'm analysing the samples obtained from the millipede. I saw what these things could do. I also want to find out if there are any nasty bugs down there."

Despite what Whyler had told him, Dad snapped, "So you're going to hang around on a crippled ship wasting valuable time waiting for results! Surely we need to get off this ship before it breaks up."

"The Empress of Incognita is unlikely to break up," Whyler assured him. "The main lattice is sound. With luck, all the bulkheads will continue to hold for several weeks. Now leave me to get on with this. If I don't get this analysed, we could be in deep trouble."

Although I wanted to leave the wreck as much as Dad, I pulled Dad's sleeve and said, "Come on. Let Carl do his job."

Eventually, Whyler emerged and began handing out pills.

Although most people swallowed them without question, Dad said, "What are these for?"

"Hopefully, they will make us all resistant to Arcadian viruses and microbes," Whyler replied.

When I showed surprise at the speed of analysis, Whyler said, "Ed and Suzanna Fyfield had already sent down probes and carried out an analysis, so the central computer confirmed the findings and manufactured what we needed very quickly. We would have had these sooner, but Whiston found out about the analysis and stole the stock."

Ignoring Whiston's theft, I latched onto the names Whyler had mentioned, "So Ed and Suzanna Fyfield are alive."

"Looks that way," Whyler replied.

When I glanced at Dad, the smile on his face proved that all the rumours were correct.

Once we'd all taken our pills, Whyler announced that he intended to use the shuttle to search for other survivors, but a mild panic broke out because someone suggested that Whyler would do what Whiston had done and steal the shuttle.

To control the rumour mill, Whyler suggested a few people went with him to ensure he returned. Dad and I were nominated as two of Whyler's *minders*.

As the shuttle was relaunched and began moving around the Empress of Incognita, everyone gasped with horror. The once-proud starship had become nothing but a wreck; in fact, it didn't take long before everyone just referred to it as The Wreck.

Partway around, everyone noted that one dome was still lit, and it was possible to see people inside waving frantically to attract our attention.

Whyler made the shuttle move closer and called the people inside, "How many of you are there?"

A weak voice said, "Just six of us."

Whyler docked and then waited for the central computer to go through procedures. Ten minutes later, the six staggered on board, and all immediately asked for water. Luckily, the shuttle had enough freshwater onboard to cater for their needs.

Not wishing to be trapped in the airlock in case of a sudden power failure, Whyler immediately reversed the docking procedure and continued looking for more survivors.

After sending message after message, Whyler finally gave up trying and returned to our airlock. On the way, he tried to be upbeat, "You will probably have noticed that some of the lifeboats were launched."

"How many?" Someone shouted out.

After interrogating the wreck's computer, Whyler said, "One hundred and fifty."

My Dad whispered, "So that means that around three thousand people escaped."

"Plus Whiston's people, these people and us," I reminded him.

~*~

Once the shuttle had docked again, it was decided that the last six rescued needed time to recover. While the droids brought us food, Carl Whyler slid down beside us. Eying the droids thoughtfully, he said, "I hope you realise that we can't take the droids with us."

Dad looked surprised, "Why not?"

"Firstly, they are linked to the ship's computer system and can't work independently. Secondly, as these droids can't deal with rough terrain, there would be no point in taking them with us even if we could modify them.."

Dad swore, "So it's back to the stone age."

"Not quite," Whyler replied. "But the cushy life we once knew is about to evaporate."

Chapter Six

Three Strange Dreams in a Row

Once we had finished eating, the lights were dimmed to conserve power, and most people fell asleep. Eventually, I nodded off too, but my dream world claimed me within seconds, and I found myself on a wooded river island. As all the trees were covered in a thick layer of Arcadian moss, the area appeared to have high rainfall.

Glancing across the river, in my dream, I saw what appeared to be hundreds of stars glistening amongst the trees. I then realised they weren't stars. They were unblinking Arcadian millipede eyes.

While I was still watching, a barrage of black spots filled the air space between the river bank and the island. I was immediately reminded of what Carl Whyler had told us. The millipedes could spit a deadly poison.

I then saw Dugal Whiston. I have to confess I experienced a whiff of schadenfreude when I saw the fear etched onto his face as more and more black spots landed on the ground not far from where he was standing.

A few seconds later, one of Whiston's gang let out a horrific scream as one of the blobs hit his face. Then, his body convulsed before he died.

In response, Whiston fired his rifle at the millipedes and ran towards an inflatable boat someone was launching on the other side of the island. As he ran, the poison blobs followed him all the way.

Two other people dived into the boat and began paddling furiously, but a third was hit on the back of her neck before she could get to the boat, and she died very quickly.

With screams of the dying echoing in my mind, I woke and reached for my diary. When I picked it up, a small light came on, and Chas said, "You awake now, Bee Bee?"

"Of course I am."

Chas said, "Just checking."

"Just checking what?"

"I've been trying to talk to you for the last half an hour, but you've been away with the fairies," Chas replied. "You've just been scribbling away in that little book."

"Scribbling away?"

Chas said, "I think you've been sleep writing."

I picked up my diary and held it so that Chas's light made it readable and then realised Chas was right. I'd already written down a complete description of my dream.

Chas suddenly reached out and grabbed my journal. When I tried to get it back, he pushed me to one side. He began glancing through my entries.

Eventually, he said, "What is this?"

As I didn't like other people reading my journal, I snapped, "What does it look like?"

Chas shrugged, "How would I know. I can't read or write."

"Can't read or write?" I echoed.

Chas changed his story, "Okay, I can read a bit but not very well. I use an electronic reader when I need to know something or read a sign."

He tossed the journal back at me contemptuously, "So, why are you scribbling in your book?"

"I always make notes," I replied. "I've done it ever since I've recovered from my accident."

"Why?"

"So I don't forget," I replied. "Since the accident, my memory isn't as good as it was."

"Tell me about the accident," Chas said.

"I've already told you," I replied.

"So, you remember that then," Chas challenged.

"Yes," I replied. "I remember telling you about the accident."

"Tell me again."

"All I remember was waking up in a hospital," I replied. "They told me I'd been in an accident. Eventually, they told me that Mum was dead."

"Tell me about the accident."

"They said it was suicide," I replied. "The authorities believe Mum drove the car into the Valles Marineris, a deep rift valley on Mars. They found a note, so they decided it was suicide. But I don't think it was…."

Chas said, "If they found a note…."

"I don't believe it," I replied. "If Mum was going to kill herself., she wouldn't have done it while Frankie and I were in the car."

"Who's Frankie?"

69

"Who *was* Frankie," I corrected. "He was Mum's new boyfriend. She left Dad and went to live with Frankie."

When tears emerged from my eyes, Chas realised he'd pushed too hard and took the conversation back to my diary, "So what were you writing?"

"I had a dream," I said. "I must have written down what I saw."

"In your sleep!"

"If you say so," I countered.

Chas said, "So, what *did* you see?"

"Dugal Whiston," I replied. "And he seemed to be in bad trouble. The millipedes were after him."

"A dream's just a dream," Chas replied dismissively. "We both hate Whiston; wishing him misfortune in a dream is not that surprising."

"It seemed very real," I said, "I *really* think I saw the giant Arcadian millipedes chasing Dugal Whiston."

Chas laughed, "I hope you're right; I hope they kill the swine."

"You don't mean that," I challenged.

"Yes, I do," Chas replied. "If he's dead, he can't kill us, can he? Couldn't happen to a nicer fella."

Instead of agreeing, I wondered if Whiston had managed to escape in his boat, but my thoughts were interrupted when I heard raised voices close by.

As Chas hadn't extinguished his torch, I saw him smile again, "Your parents are arguing again. They've been at it off and on for hours."

As I hadn't heard anything, I said, "What about?"

"Your step Mum thinks your Dad was having an affair with Suzanna Fyfield," Chas replied. He added, "I told you he was, and now your step-mum has realised the truth."

Despite what I knew, I leapt to Dad's defence, "That's the trouble with people. They always think the worst and go around spreading rumours."

Chas held his hand up, "Okay … Okay … Calm down. You may well be right. It's just nasty rumours."

~*~

I must have fallen asleep again because the dreams returned, but Dugal Whiston didn't feature in them this time. Instead, I saw Mary reaching out and picking shiny berries from a strange-looking bush and dropping them into a woven container.

Once the container was full, Mary emptied the contents onto a table and began puncturing them. She put them on a plastimetal tray over an open fire and heated the berries until they went hard.

Then, she stitched the bead-like berries onto a peaked cap. Mary handed me the hat and smiled at me, "You must wear this all the time to protect yourself from the Great Ones."

"Who are the Great Ones?"

Mary smiled, "You will learn that shortly."

When I awoke, Chas shone his torch on me again, "You've had another dream, haven't you?"

"How do you know?"

Chas picked up my diary and handed it to me.

Once again, I had already recorded my dream about Mary.

"Why do you use an old fashioned book to make notes?" Chas said.

For once, I didn't try to disguise the truth, "Because Dad goes through my things when he thinks I'm not watching and checks up on me. He says it's because he's worried that I'll do something stupid like Mum did."

"That doesn't answer the question," Chas said. "Why have you gone primitive and started handwriting things?"

"Because it's easier to hide small books," I replied. "I don't want Dad being able to check up on everything I do—don't you think I'm entitled to some privacy?"

Chas nodded, "Too right."

~*~

The third dream was the strangest of them all, and I found myself in an underground city with weird green lighting. The tunnels that formed the city were patrolled by giant six-legged ant-like creatures, and I later discovered they were Arcadian wolves.

My dream took me into a side cavern where what looked like substantial plastimetal bags were hanging from the ceiling. It took me deeper into the cave, and I realised I could see through the bags when there was a light behind them. Inside, there were juvenile Arcadian wolves busily developing. It was only then that I realised the bags were artificial wombs.

My mind took me into another cave system. This time the grow-sacks contained juvenile giant Arcadian millipedes, identical to the one that had come back with the shuttle.

While I was still watching, I was transported to another cell, and I saw Dugal Whiston and the remnants of his gang chained to what looked like operating tables. Hovering directly over them were four balls of light.

I don't know how I knew, but I realised that the light balls were controlled by the Great Ones, who were in the process of interrogating the captives.

I felt it when Whiston's mind partially collapsed, and he agreed to serve the Great Ones if they spared his life. Then I heard the light balls instruct him to go down river and capture as many survivors as possible.

Opening his eyes, Whiston said, "So you want me to round them up and bring them back here, eh?"

One of the light balls said, "Correct."

"You will also kill the one who's called Bee-Bee. He is a danger to us," a mind voice said.

"Great," Whiston replied, "Killing Bee Bee will be my pleasure. I'd also like to settle a few other scores at the same time."

"No," the mind voice snapped, "Only kill the one called Bee Bee, and you will not harm the rest if at all possible."

Whiston scowled, "Why not?"

"If you want to live, you will obey us," one of the light balls said.

As Whiston regained some control of his faculties, his obnoxious personality returned. The scowl turned into a look of contempt, "And what will you do if I don't?"

Both Whiston and I were immediately transported to a strange-looking chamber. I didn't feel scared because I seemed to be hovering over Whiston, not quite in the room but still present. I was a ghost floating above Whiston's head.

After a few seconds, one of the end walls began to shake. Then a head broke through the wall, followed by a section of the torso. I was staring at it; I realised it was similar to the Arcadian wolf I'd seen in the artificial wombs.

Catching sight of Whiston, the giant grub let out a rattle and then began easing its way further into its feeding chamber.

Whiston squared up to the beast aggressively, but his resolve melted as the grub sent out a mental message, "Fight me if you will, but I will make you suffer. Submit, and I will cut off your head and make your death very swift."

The grub hauled more of its body into the feeding chamber. It snapped its mandibles as if looking forward to feasting on Whiston's body. As the huge grub continued to advance, Whiston realised he was about to die a horrible death and pleaded for his life, "Please don't let it kill me!"

The grub stopped its advance a moment later and just glared at Whiston. But it kept on snapping its mandibles as if ready to recommence its attack if the Great Ones permitted it.

Realising that his fate still hung in the balance, Whiston repeated, "Please don't let it kill me!"

As if in answer, one of the light balls appeared and said, "Your life will only be spared if you swear an oath of allegiance to the Great Ones."

Grasping at the straw being offered, Whiston said, "Yes, yes. Anything! I don't want to die."

The light ball said, "Kneel!"

Reluctantly, Whiston dropped to his knees.

The light ball gave Whiston his oath, and he repeated it, "I swear to the Great Ones, I will obey all their commands and will be their brave soldier at all times."

The light ball said, "Your pledge is accepted, but if you break your oath, you will be sent back to this chamber or one like it. Do you understand?"

Whiston nodded, and he was returned to the bench he had been lying on. Like a fly on the ceiling, I was staring down at him.

Whiston looked straight at me and pointed, "Bee-Bee is there now."

The light balls suddenly turned and moved towards me. A second later, I felt something forcing its way into my mind and guessed that the light balls had detected my presence and attempted to take me over.

Fearing that I might end up like Dugal Whiston, I fought back. The next thing I knew, I was back on the Empress, my arms were flailing at an invisible enemy, and Chas had his torch trained on me again, "Three bad dreams in a row, which must be some sort of record. What did you dream *this* time?"

"Dugal Whiston has been captured, and he's agreed to serve the Great Ones," I told him.

"Then the Great Ones tried to take me over," I explained. "But I escaped."

"Who are the Great Ones?" Chas demanded.

I shook my head, "I've no idea, but they seem very powerful. They want me dead."

Instead of taking my comment seriously, Chas sniffed. Then, he said, "You're getting seriously weird, you know that, Bee Bee. Maybe the bad air in here is getting to you."

~*~

After lights-on, Carl Whyler appeared and gave his morning briefing. It was designed to create hope, and the upside was he'd hinted that the downshuttle to Arcadia wasn't far off.

Once he'd finished, Dad and Chas began talking to the rest of the survivors.

As Mary was standing at the back, I moved in, took her to one side and said, "I heard you and Dad arguing."

Mary was dismissive, "It was nothing. I was jealous, but your Dad has assured me that he's *not* been having an affair with Suzanna Fyfield."

My mind took me straight back to the accusation that Ed Fyfield had made when he'd caught us leaving the observation area. I was tempted to say something to Mary, but I chickened out again.

While I was still thinking, Mary said, "In any case, how could he be having an affair unless Suzanna Fyfield was bringing him out of suspension illegally so that they could have a dalliance."

The comment made me think back to when we'd come out of suspension; Dad had always been awake first, and he'd also seemed to be fully recovered before anyone else. Although he'd denied having an affair with Suzanna Fyfield, if she had been allowing him out of suspension so that they could be together, it would answer a lot of questions.

Still not wanting to cause trouble, I changed the subject and told Mary about my last dream and her appearance in it. I then said, "What d'you think it means?"

"Very little I should think," Mary replied in an off-handed manner. "I've never heard of the Great Ones, and I don't know anything about these strange berries that I was turning into beads."

Chapter Seven

Downshuttle to Arcadia

Two days later, Carl Whyler announced we were going to downshuttle. But, he added, "Before we do, let's find some guns and ammunition."

Once he'd located arms lockers Whiston and his mob had not vandalised, he unlocked them and pointed at the rifles and pistols, "Take those and plenty of ammunition."

As the passengers followed his instructions, my Dad grabbed a rifle, a couple of handguns and boxes of ammunition and passed them to me. He ordered, "Do not load them or point them at anyone."

Whyler relaunched the shuttle two hours later, with everyone packed in like sardines. Those who hadn't seen how badly the Empress had been damaged stared at the stricken starship in disbelief and began thinking hard about the future.

During descent, Whyler announced that he was deliberately excluding the last two landing sites because he didn't want to run into Arcadian millipedes or Whiston and his trigger-happy gang. As he mentioned Whiston, I thought about my strange dreams again. If Whiston intended to kill me, I knew I would need to be very careful.

Once the shuttle had re-entered Arcadia's atmosphere, Whyler began checking for distress signals from the escape pods. Then, picking up on a large cluster, he instructed the shuttle to land on a large outcrop of rock some distance from the first cluster of escape pods.

Being close to Whyler, Dad whispered, "Why have we landed here, Carl?"

"Common sense," Whyler replied. "If any people down there are like Dugal Whiston, they might start shooting at us. Besides, I've got a bad feeling about this."

I said, "A bad feeling about what?"

Whyler pointed towards the leather winged creatures circling the area, "That doesn't look good, does it? They look like vultures."

After taking off again and manoeuvring the shuttle over the landing site, Whyler engaged the shuttle's external loud hailers. Instead of getting the reaction he'd hoped, the loudspeakers just made the birdlike creatures rise en mass.

They began to mob the shuttle, hitting the sides and making it wobble.

As some of the creatures flashed past the windows, a passenger gasped out, "They're pterodactyls."

As most of Earth's History and the Theory of Evolution had been removed from the curriculum in schools on Mars Base five, I said, "What's a pterodactyl?"

Someone pointed out of the window, "One of **them**!"

Someone else shouted, "They can't be pterodactyls; they became extinct millions of years ago."

"Convergent evolution," someone else shouted back.

Turning to my Dad, I said, "What the hell are they talking about? Pterodactyls and convergent evolution?"

For once, he wasn't stumped, "Convergent evolution is when different species develop into a similar body shape reacting to their natural environment. For instance, some cacti and succulents look very similar, but they are from different species, but the conditions have made them adapt to survive. If those things out there look like pterodactyls, it's because natural selection has made them that way."

When I frowned, he admitted, "I'd forgotten that the schools you attended weren't allowed to teach you about Charles Darwin and the Origins of Species. If you remind me, I'll tell you all about it later."

As the pterodactyl mobbing worsened, Whyler made the shuttle retreat and looked for other landing sites. After visiting five separate sites and finding Arcadian pterodactyls circling all of them, Whyler set the shuttle down well away from the last scene of carnage.

First, he dealt with the panic running through the passengers. Holding up one of the pills he'd handed out on the Empress, Whyler said, "That's why I gave you a pill while we were on the Empress, and it should help everyone combat Arcadian infections."

Whyler began handing out second pills. After swallowing her second pill, Mary whispered, "How do we know the drug he's given us will work?"

Whyler overheard her and came over, "We don't know. All we can do is hope."

After finding nothing but corpses at the five main landing sites, Carl Whyler appeared to lose interest in looking for other escape pods on the mainland and instructed the shuttle to head towards the coast. Once there, he began hugging the coastline.

Eventually, four islands appeared at the mouth of a large river. After carefully inspecting all the islands, Whyler moved towards the largest island, which seemed to have a freshwater lake at its centre.

As the shuttle moved over the largest island, Whyler scanned for hostile fauna and then put down. A question was immediately thrown at him, "Why have you landed here?"

Instead of answering the question, Whyler flipped a few switches, and a large screen popped out of one of the walls and displayed the external terrain. Not far away, there were several escape pods.

More importantly, there were signs of life. People were walking around, and there were no signs of the circling Arcadian pterodactyls. Realising the group who'd dropped on the island hadn't suffered the fate of the other groups, a cheer ran out. A few seconds later, voices came in over the shuttle's communications system, and Carl Whyler began exchanging pleasantries.

Eventually, Ed and Suzanna Fyfield boarded and welcomed us to North Island. Seeing Suzanna Fyfield, I thought about the argument I'd overheard and glanced toward Dad.

As he was staring at Suzanna with unconcealed interest, I began to feel very uneasy. During my life at Mars Base 5, infidelity and partner breakups had been only too familiar. I thought about my earlier conversation with Mary. She'd accepted Dad's assurances that he hadn't been having an affair with Suzanna Fyfield, but the expression on his face said otherwise.

I also recalled Ed Fyfield's comments when we'd come out of the observation room on the Empress of Incognita. He'd accused Dad and Suzanna of suspension bed-hopping. There could be little doubt in my mind that he'd been telling the truth.

Once the Fyfields had welcomed us, we were asked to vacate the shuttle because they said it would be needed to make more trips to the Empress of Incognita to claim any remaining supplies before the shuttle's fuel ran out.

When most people were reluctant to leave the shuttle, Ed Fyfield said, "The Empress sent down a supply pod to our location, so we have enough spare tents to house you all."

Accepting his orders, we left the shuttle taking the few possessions and guns we'd pillaged from the Empress of Incognita with us. We were pleased to discover that several multi-berth tents were erected within minutes, and my parents, Chas and I swiftly claimed one. Once inside, I ran a hand over the roof and walls of the tent. As they were smooth, I guessed they were made from plastimetal, similar to the food production sphere on the Empress.

Once we'd dumped our belongings, Ed Fyfield took us to an open campfire and introduced us to a large group of people sitting around it.

He then went to a primitive barbeque that someone had built out of beach stones and extracted a skewer with food on it. Pulling out a homemade Bowie sword, Ed

Fyfield swiftly chopped the meat up and began distributing it to the newcomers.

As he did so, I cast a glance in Chas's direction. The *Butcher* had made himself a new knife, and I couldn't help but wonder how long it would be before he started using it to reinforce his position.

As I couldn't remember the last time I'd eaten a decent meal, I sank my teeth into the offering without thinking about what I was eating. A few swallows later, I glanced at Dad and said, "Any idea what this is?"

One of the established group cut in, "What does it taste like, young man?"

"A bit like chicken," I replied.

"Then, as far as you are concerned, it's chicken," the other man said. "Now eat or go hungry!"

As I was still ravenous, I didn't ask any more questions, and I just carried on eating. A few hours later, I discovered we'd been eating a giant Arcadian millipede that a hunting party had shot in the Arcadian mangroves.

Once we'd finished eating, Ed Fyfield walked over to Carl Whyler and started talking to him. Although I couldn't hear all the conversation, I caught the gist. Ed Fyfield was trying to establish how safe it would be to fly back to the wreck for more supplies.

Whyler left him in little doubt concerning the terrible conditions inside the wreck. He explained that the only sensible approach would be to allow the auxiliary computer to carry out a complete check followed by a period of monitoring. He said that no one should return until safe areas had been established.

Ed Fyfield didn't sound happy with the idea but eventually gave in when Carl Whyler showed him some of the photographs he'd taken.

Once he'd completed his discussions with Whyler, Fyfield gathered together the shuttle passengers and said, "What I am about to tell you will upset some people, but I'm going to be straight with you."

After a deliberately long pause, he added, "Some people think we will be rescued, but I think that is highly unlikely."

Ed Fyfield reminded me of what I already knew. As the mine attacks had forced the Empress of Incognita into an unexplored wormhole, no one would know where we were. Even if they guessed, it was improbable that the authorities would allow a rescue mission until the wormhole branch was deemed safe, which could take years.

Ed Fyfield said, "We must presume that we are marooned and do our best to survive. It means we will have to plant crops and hunt wild game."

After letting the message sink in, Ed Fyfield added, "I will give you work details later."

Then, as he stood up to leave, he continued, "One other thing. The Arcadian day-night cycle is three times longer than an Earth day-night cycle. This will mean that a lot of the work will occur at night. It will also mean that you will have to day-sleep. But I have no doubt we will get used to it."

I thought that Ed Fyfield's talk was upsetting but truthful. But just as we were about to go to our tents, a loud voice said, "Who put you in charge, Fyfield? You are no longer a ship's officer; you are no different from us."

Ed Fyfield pulled out his Bowie sword and moved towards Loud Voice. After touching the sharp blade to Loud Voice's neck, Ed Fyfield said, "D'you want to fight me for leadership?"

The Adam's apple in Loud Voice's neck began to jerk involuntarily.

"**Well**?" Ed Fyfield demanded. "D'you want to fight me?"

Loud Voice shook his head because he realised he wouldn't be spared if he accepted Fyfield's challenge and lost the fight.

I thought about the fight between Ed Fyfield and Dugal Whiston. If they came head to head again, would Fyfield still win if there was another clash?

Ignoring the head shake the other man had made, Ed Fyfield repeated, "Well! D'you want to fight me?"

Loud Mouth shook his head again and said, "Of course, I don't want to fight you."

Retracting the sword slightly, Ed Fyfield replied, "For your information, the others elected me to be the leader before you arrived. Are you happy with that?"

Loud Voice once again confirmed that he wasn't challenging Fyfield's role in the group.

Satisfied he'd cowed the other man into submission, Ed Fyfield added, "If anyone doesn't want to stay on these islands, they are free to leave at any time."

"But if anyone leaves, they can't expect to take any of the equipment we may bring down from the Empress of

Incognita using the shuttle. What this group brings down, this group keeps. No one will be allowed to steal the family silver. If you leave, you will have nothing other than the clothes on your backs."

Chapter Eight

Dreams of Akbar

The dreams started the instant I climbed into my sleeping bag, and I felt as if I was coming out of the suspension unit again because I found myself inside the strange dark pyramid once more with a bright light at the top. Only the bony arms and hands reaching out to grab me were missing.

Then the mental images changed, and a face I'd only seen once before came into my mind. It was the face of the person who'd issued the warning, "You are in great danger, Bee Bee. Choose your friends carefully."

To be honest, it was a face that I find hard to describe. It was like a computer-generated image, and yet, it wasn't. It seemed human, and yet I knew it wasn't.

Like the other dreams, when the man spoke, it felt like the sounds were coming from inside my head. The face said, "Why are you here?"

Instead of answering the question, I asked, "Who are you?"

"I don't have a name," the voice said.

"No name?"

There was a slight pause; the voice added, "I can tell that names matter to your species. Very well, you can call me eh, eh, Akbar?"

When I mentally nodded, Akbar repeated his question, "Why are you here?"

Then I felt him probing; it was like a fat slug slip-sliding over my brain. It was similar to the probing that the Great Ones had attempted.

Akbar repeated, "Why are you here?"

"We didn't want to be here," I replied. "We've been shipwrecked on Arcadia."

"Arcadia?"

"That is what we call this planet," I explained.

"Why Arcadia?"

I shrugged, "I don't know. Someone told me that in mythology, Arcadia was supposed to be a mysterious place, full of strange creatures."

Akbar considered my answer, "Maybe the name is apt."

"In what way?"

"There are creatures on this planet that you will find strange," Akbar replied.

"What strange creatures?" I demanded. "Are you referring to the Arcadian millipedes?"

"There are many other creatures on Arcadia," Akbar replied.

"And who are you, Akbar?"

"I am about to tell you," Akbar said. "I am one of the guardians of this planet. But my role is complicated and limited, Bee Bee. I have to keep an eye on the Great Ones to make sure they don't escape, but I can only warn people like you to stay away; I can't physically intervene."

"Who are the Great Ones?" I asked, "And why are you watching them?"

Akbar said, "The lands surrounding the river and the high lands beyond are a reservation, and the Great Ones have been exiled there."

"Exiled? Why?"

Akbar said. "The Great Ones were sent to this planet for security reasons. This planet is far from the rest of our culture. Under our laws, execution is not possible. So sending them here seemed a sensible solution; they were banished to repent for their war crimes."

"So they are in prison!"

"That is a simple way of looking at it," Akbar agreed.

I said, "Did the Great Ones create the minefield that destroyed our starship?"

"Perhaps", Akbar replied. "Then again, perhaps not. There were a lot of weapons used before the Great Ones surrendered."

There was a long pause, and then Akbar said, "Your people plan to travel up the river."

I was surprised, *"Do they?"*

"Yes," Akbar replied, *"They must **not** do this!"*

"Why not?"

"Because the creatures the Great Ones control in the reservation will either kill or enslave your people if they go there."

The comment made me recall one of my other dreams when the Great Ones had instructed Dugal Whiston to make our group prisoners. I then thought about Whiston's response and his desire for revenge.

Akbar latched onto my thoughts and said, "You must not dismiss your other dreams. Other guardians work independently from me, and I do not doubt that they have been contacting you too, although it is obvious they have not been as direct as I have been."

"Why do you work independently?"

Akbar gave me a wry smile, "The Great Ones were only beaten because they were universally feared, and the allies fought against them. Unfortunately, the allies who defeated them were from many factions. Now that the common enemy is beaten, the old rivalries have renewed."

"Why do the Great Ones want to kill me?"

"I would have thought that was obvious," Akbar replied.

"Not to me, it isn't," I said.

"Most of your people in your group have closed minds," Akbar said. "There are only two others, other than yourself, who have open minds."

"Two others? Who are they?" I asked.

"I'm afraid I can't tell you that," Akbar replied.

"Why not?"

"Because I am not permitted to tell you," Akbar replied

Realising I wouldn't get the information, I changed tack and said, "Why is my mind open?"

"Your accident opened parts of your mind and closed others," Akbar replied.

"So the Great Ones want to kill me because they perceive me as a danger?"

"Without a doubt," Akbar agreed.

"Why do the Great Ones want to take our people prisoner?"

"The Great Ones are parasites; they either live in the bodies of other species or implant their essence in other species so that they can control them. They see your people as being useful to them because you have well-developed brains and hands."

He added, "They have enslaved other species, and they will do the same to yours."

A moment later, Akbar sent me an image of a giant Arcadian millipede and said, "This is one species they have enslaved. From what you have said, I believe you call them Arcadian Millipedes."

The image triggered my dream memories of the aliens I'd seen in the strange artificial wombs and the beast that Carl Whyler had accidentally brought back on the shuttle.

Picking up on my thoughts, Akbar said, "The one you call Carl Whyler is lucky to be alive. "

"Why?"

"Because the creatures that you have named giant Arcadian millipedes are under the control of the Great Ones can spit a deadly poison," Akbar said, "If it goes on the skin of your people, it will probably kill in a matter of minutes. Carl Whyler only survived because the creature that came back with him had exhausted its venom on other victims."

Akbar then sent me an image of a six-legged creature with huge mandibles that looked vaguely ant-like. Akbar then said, "These creatures, are equivalent of earth wolves. In the wild they hunt in massive packs."

"I said, "Arcadian wolves."

"For simplicity, let's call them that," Akbar agreed. "The Arcadian wolves are also controlled by the Great Ones and are very dangerous."

My thoughts shot back to the previous dream I'd had about Whiston and his escape from the river island.

I hadn't seen any Arcadian wolves, but I'd seen plenty of giant millipedes. I thought about Whiston's capture and the threat to feed Whiston to the wolf larvae.

Reading my thoughts, Akbar said, "The one you call Whiston took to a boat, but it didn't do him much good because, as you know, he was still captured by the Great Ones."

As Akbar triggered a sense of unease in my mind, I said, "What will the Great Ones do to Whiston and the others with him?"

"They will evaluate them," Akbar replied. "If they are deemed suitable, they will be allowed to live."

"Suitable? Suitable for what?"

"I've already told you," Akbar replied. "If they make good, enslaved people, the Great Ones will look for ways of converting the human race. As I said before, the Great Ones are parasites and have learned to enslave and control many animals and plants in the prison zone."

"What if Whiston and his people are deemed unsuitable?"

"They will be killed. Growing wolves like fresh meat. If Whiston and his associates don't prove themselves, they are likely to be fed to the Arcadian wolf larvae."

My thoughts immediately recalled the earlier dream and the cell that Whiston had been sent to for his mock execution.

Akbar picked up on my thoughts again and said, "Ah! I see you already know about that."

"Yes," I replied. "In that dream, Dugal Whiston agreed to help the Great Ones catch us. What will happen if he does?"

"If he catches you, he will kill you," Akbar replied. "The rest will sufferer the same fate as all the other animals that once roamed free in their reservation."

"And what fate is that?"

"I've told you, "Akbar replied. "You will be enslaved, and the Great Ones will also try to selectively breed from your stock. Once they have managed to create a human/Great One hybrid, your people will be surplus to requirements."

When I frowned, unbelieving, Akbar added, "You saw the breeding pouches. The Arcadian wolves and millipedes in the reservation were once free; now, they're the Great One's slaves. They do as they are told. There are still some wild wolves and millipedes in the inaccessible areas, but the Great Ones have taken over most wolf and millipede colonies in the valley and the plateau beyond."

I thought about the food I'd been eating, but I didn't have to ask Akbar about millipedes on North Island because he said, "Don't worry. The millipedes you are hunting for food are not the same species as those in the prison zone. The ones you are hunting can spit poison, but their venom is very mild compared to the millipedes in the river zone and plateaux."

When my mind expressed surprise, Akbar said, "The Great Ones have deliberately bred the dangerous ones to become their soldiers."

"Bred them?"

"Selective breeding," Akbar replied. "Like your people did to dogs and horses."

"So who are these Great Ones," I asked.

"You cannot see them for what they are," Akbar replied. "As I told you, they are skilled at hiding their true selves within other flora or fauna; I repeat, they are parasites."

Akbar added, "Be careful. Someone you trust will very shortly let you down."

When I awoke, Chas said, "You've been screaming out and doing that sleep writing thing again."

I reached for my diary and checked it and discovered I'd written three pages describing my contact with Akbar.

~*~

When Nigel, one of Ed Fyfield's men, woke us up, it was still night. He took us to a mess tent for breakfast. I was tempted to tell Dad and Mary about the strange dream I'd had and my latest sleep-writing, but Akbar's warning made me hold my tongue. Then Nigel appeared and ordered us to join a work party.

"So let's get moving. Work Party 4." Nigel chivvied.

Dad's jaw dropped, "Work party?"

Nigel didn't mince words, "Ed told you we have to plant crops. Come with me."

We were all presented with homemade plastimetal spades and hatchets. I could tell Dad wasn't impressed. As he'd been used to ordering droids to carry out manual work all his life, he had no desire to change the status quo.

After a short walk, Nigel showed us a shrub-covered area that had been pegged out into a square and instructed us on the basics of simple agriculture. Then, he told us to clear the area and suggested that a controlled burn was the best start.

As Nigel began building kindling to ignite the Arcadian brambles, I saw a bush similar to the one I had seen in my dreams and swiftly picked the berries. Having nothing to put them in, I pulled down a large leaf from another plant, wrapped the berries, and then pushed the package into my pocket.

I'd barely finished before Nigel's fire took hold and swiftly ripped through the undergrowth. After the fire had done its work, Nigel told us to stamp out the embers and dig. When he was satisfied that we'd removed the old roots and prepared the land properly, we started planting.

By the time we'd finished, I was aching all over. Dad was complaining too. Within a matter of hours, he announced he was going to join a hunting group.

I wasn't that surprised. As Dad loved guns and disliked manual work, it was logical for him to try to change. However, I soon realised he had an ulterior motive.

Suzanna Fyfield was leading his hunting group and wondered if Akbar's predictions were about to come true. *Someone you trust will very shortly let you down.*

~*~

After I had eaten my evening meal, more Arcadian millipede bulked out by processed vegetables stored in the escape pods; I fished out the berries I'd found, pierced them as I'd seen in my dream and put them on a hot stone near to the fire. Within seconds they hardened. I was on the point of wrapping them up again when Dad came over and said, "You're not going to eat those, are you?"

I shook my head, "I've turned them into beads."

"What for?"

"It's an experiment," I replied.

Dad frowned, "Well, don't eat them. They could be poisonous."

He walked away, and as I was tired, I went to bed.

Akbar came to me within an instant of my head touching the pillow and said, "I am glad to see you have created the beads, and you must now stitch them onto a cap and wear it at all times."

"Why?"

"If you don't, the Great Ones will try to invade your mind."

"Like *you* do?" I challenged.

Akbar became abrasive, "I only communicate. I have no desire to take you over."

He added, "The hat will not stop the Great Ones or me talking to you, but the Great Ones will not be able to invade your mind. The beads will hold them back; you will not be at their mercy if you wear the beaded hat."

The comment made me think about the episode when the balls of light had tried to do just that. Reading my thoughts, Akbar said, "I'm glad that you have experienced their power because I now know that you will believe me."

Akbar continued, "Your father has volunteered to be a hunter?"

I mentally nodded, "Yes, he has. But how did you know?"

I saw a smile form on Akbar's face, "Your mind is not the only one I am reading."

"So you can read my father's thoughts," I challenged.

"No, I can't," Akbar replied. "I have told you there are two other people whose minds are open to me. Your father's mind is not one of them."

His demeanour then became more forceful, "I warned you. *No one must go upriver.*"

"I'll do my best to warn them," I said. "But...."

"But what?"

"I'm only young," I told Akbar. "It is unlikely they will believe I am receiving warnings from you. Can't you contact Ed Fyfield? He is our leader."

Akbar said, "I can't mind-link with Ed Fyfield. You must tell him what I have told you."

~*~

As I awoke, Chas said, "You've just had another dream, haven't you?"

"Akbar has told me to warn Ed Fyfield that he mustn't send anyone upriver."

When Chas let out a slight laugh, I said, "Have I said something funny?"

"You're in your own little world," Chas replied. "Aren't you?"

"What's that meant to mean?"

"While you have been thinking about these dreams, everything else has passed you by."

"Eh?"

Chas shook his head in disbelief, "Everyone's been talking about it."

About what?"

"Ed Fyfield has been ratified by the General Council as our leader," Chas replied.

"I know that!"

"Did you know that River and Valley surrounding is now called the Fyfield Valley and Fyfield River in his honour?"

"You're joking!"

"No," Chas replied. "More importantly, the General Council has also approved a plan to explore the Fyfield Valley."

"You keep talking about this General Council," I said, "So when did the General Council come into being?"

Chas shrugged, "No idea, but it doesn't really concern us."

"Why not?"

"We're too young to vote," Chas replied.

"I still need to see him," I said.

"Good luck with that then," Chas sniggered, "The decision to go upriver has already been made, and if you go and see Ed with dream stories, he'll probably tell you you're insane."

Even though I knew that Chas was right, I rolled out of bed and went to Ed Fyfield's tent, but I didn't go in because I thought I might disturb his sleep.

While I was still thinking about my next move, Ed Fyfield strode into view, and his first comment knocked me for six. Barely glancing at me, his voice became highly contemptuous, and he asked, "What do you want?"

"Could I have a word with you?" I stuttered.

"If you want to join a hunting party, the answer is no," Fyfield replied. "We now have all the hunters we need."

"No, it wasn't that," I said. "It's just that I don't think you should go upriver. The millipedes upriver are a different species and highly venomous," I said.

"How did you know we were going upriver?" Fyfield demanded. "Did your father tell you?"

"No," I replied. "I had a bad dream about it, and I was warned that you'd be in danger."

Ed Fyfield burst out laughing, "You had a dream! What are you? The Oracle of Delphi?"

I decided that attack was the best means of defence, "Aren't you worried about your sister being killed?"

"My sister is her own person," Ed Fyfield laughed. "If I tried to stop her going upriver, she'd do it just to defy me."

"So you are not going to stop her?"

"No," Ed Fyfield replied. "I'm not. Her hunting party will be leaving shortly. And, for your information, when I have time, I will be joining one of the expeditions."

Realising I'd failed in my mission, I beat a hasty retreat.

Once I returned to my tent, Chas asked me how it went.

I shrugged and admitted Ed Fyfield wasn't interested in my dreams.

As I had nothing better to do that night, I decided to stitch the beads I'd made to the peaked cap I'd acquired. I hit the first hurdle because I lacked a needle and thread.

I thought back to my dreams and went out and collected a thin grass-like weed. Once back in the tent, I used the weed to attach the beads to my hat.

I pulled the cap on and was amazed at the difference it made to my mental state. Ever since I'd down shuttled to Arcadia, my mind had been cluttered with strange sounds and images, and now it was crystal clear.

Chapter Nine

The Battle of North Island

After two days of toil, my Dad went off with one of the hunting teams. Fearful that he would go upriver, I resolved to speak to him, but he hadn't returned when I'd finished work.

So, I went to bed, and Akbar came into my mind almost immediately; he sent me an image of my Dad with Suzanna Fyfield. While I was watching, an Arcadian millipede appeared, but instead of attacking them, the beast presented them with a huge leaf containing exotic fruit.

More importantly, the body language that Suzanna Fyfield was displaying suggested that she didn't just want a platonic relationship with my Dad.

Seeingly unperturbed by the millipede's presence, Suzanna selected one of the fruits and bit into it. As she did so, I was reminded of an archaic myth: Eve supposedly being tempted by the serpent and eating the forbidden fruit.

As the millipede brought more fruit, Akbar's mind image pulled back and permitted me to see where Dad and Suzanna were sitting. They were in a cave system, illuminated by a strange greenish light. As I'd seen the green light before, I knew they were with the Great Ones. I also saw one of the ship's communicators on a table. As

I watched, it sounded, and Suzanna began talking to someone. Although I couldn't figure out who she was talking to, I wondered if it was Ed Fyfield, her brother. Did he know she was with the Great Ones?

After absorbing the mental transmission for some time, I realised that Akbar was tapping into Suzanna's thoughts and concluded that she must have been one of the other two people with open minds.

Shocked by what I was seeing, I said, "Why didn't you tell me Suzanna and my Dad would run away together, Akbar?"

Akbar let out a mental tut as if disgusted by my comment, "I am neither your servant nor your babysitter. I cannot check on everything you humans do. My duties cover many things. Besides, I have told you I can't intervene. I do not have the power to do so."

Ignoring Akbar's snipe at my expense, I said, "Presumably, when they said they were going hunting, they intended to meet the Great Ones."

"It would appear that way," Akbar agreed.

While my mind was absorbing the unwelcome information, Akbar confirmed my worst fears by saying, "As the Great Ones appear to be treating them well. I believe that your father and Suzanna Fyfield are unlikely to return."

After listening to Dad and Suzanna's conversation via Akbar's mind link for a while longer, I realised Dad had lied to Mary for months. It was also evident that Dad's transfer to the hunting party had been an excuse to be with Suzanna Fyfield and escape from Mary and our camp. The conversation also implied that Ed Fyfield may have sent them upriver as ambassadors. But why? I thought about the ship's communicator again. Everything suggested that Ed Fyfield knew where they were and was being briefed by Suzanna.

Akbar's dream message showed me images of escape pods that had crashed through the trees and landed in the territory controlled by the Great Ones.

I saw people in a vast cave working on projects. Akbar said, "The Great Ones realised that the survivors are capable of great dexterity because of their hands, and they have been set to work producing things that the millipedes cannot do."

Struck by the difference between the majority and the regal life offered to Dad and Suzanna Fyfield, I queried it.

"The Great Ones read the minds of the majority," Akbar replied. "As Suzanna Fyfield was the most senior member of the Empress of Incognita's crew to survive other than her brother, the Great Ones have elevated her above the rest. When it is necessary to give orders to the others, Suzanna acts as a go-between."

"What about my father?"

"He is being treated as Suzanna Fyfield's consort," Akbar replied.

I suddenly felt angry because he'd deserted Mary. Then, as if to answer my thoughts, Akbar predicted, "Your father will live a life of luxury until Suzanna Fyfield tires of him."

"Then what?"

"I can't predict his fate," Akbar replied.

When I awoke, Chas gave me the usual flippant interrogation. As I didn't want to say anything to Mary because I hoped the dream that Akbar had sent me was false, I confided in Chas instead.

As Chas liked conspiracy theories, he said, "It sounds as if Ed Fyfield knows they have already joined the Great Ones. On the other hand, maybe he sent you away with a flea in your ear because he doesn't want you snitching on his sister. If your Dad is cheating on your stepmother, maybe Ed doesn't want it to become public knowledge just yet."

In the end, I decided not to say anything to anyone else because I thought that Dad might come back to his senses and return to camp.

~*~

The following day, Dad still hadn't returned, but someone came to our tent and handed a letter to Mary. Instead of talking to me, she disappeared.

As Mary was working alongside me on the newly reclaimed land, I finally broached the subject of Dad's absence, and she finally gave me the bad news.

After handing me the letter, Mary said, "Your Dad has been lying about Suzanna Fyfield. He's been carrying on an affair with Suzanna Fyfield for months."

After reading the letter and thinking about Akbar's dreams, I realised that my worst fears had come to fruition. My mind then conjured up images of Suzanna

Fyfield releasing my Dad from his suspension unit early so they could be together

~*~

After work had finished, it was another groundhog day; tired, I went to bed. But this time, instead of thinking about Dad, I had a dream about Dugal Whiston.

Whiston was paddling down the river heading for our island; I woke with a start.

As I didn't like Ed Fyfield and suspected he was playing some sort of devious game, I swiftly spoke to Chas, told him what I'd dreamed and said, "So what do I do? Do I tell Fyfield or not?"

Chas let out a raspberry, "I'll say this for you; you're a glutton for punishment."

"So I don't tell, Ed Fyfield," I said.

"That's up to you," Chas replied evasively.

"But what if Whiston is coming for us?"

Chas shrugged, "These dreams of yours seem very farfetched."

"So, do I ignore the dream?"

Chas shrugged again, "Go and see Fyfield if you think you have to but don't expect the red carpet treatment. He'll probably send you away with a flea in your ear again. especially if he's cosying up to the Great Ones."

In the end, I ignored Chas's unhelpful comments, and I went to Ed Fyfield's tent despite my doubts and the rebuff I'd received last time.

Luckily, he was still awake and sitting around a fire with several other people.

As I approached, he pulled out his Bowie sword and began cutting up the flesh of an Arcadian millipede he'd shot during a hunt. It confirmed what I'd already suspected, Ed Fyfield's close associates were always rewarded with extra food to keep them loyal.

As before, he greeted me with a gruff, "What do you want this time?"

Undeterred, I told him that Dugal Whiston would attack North Island.

I could tell he was about to send me away, but Carl Whyler intervened. "It might be a false alarm, but I think we should prepare our defences."

"Why? Because this young fool claims to have psychic gifts?" Ed Fyfield demanded.

"No," Carl Whyler snapped, "Because Dugal Whiston is a nasty bit of work, and he might want to steal all the equipment we've salvaged from the Empress."

Whyler pointed to his arm, "In case you've forgotten, Dugal Whiston shot me, and I don't want to risk that he'll try the same again."

Ed Fyfield gave me a stern look, "Okay, clever dick, prove how good you are. When will Dugal Whiston attack us, and which way will he come."

"He's already coming downriver," I replied, "He'll be here within the hour, and he's going to land in Top Bay."

"Come on," Whyler snapped. "Let's get our guns and get up to Top Bay."

Without waiting for Ed Fyfield to comment, Whyler tapped me on one arm and said, "Come on, Bee Bee."

After rushing to his tent, he picked up two rifles and ammunition and gave me one and a box of cartridges. Then, he began rounding up more people to help. Within a matter of minutes, ten people set off to Top Bay.

Ed Fyfield came along, but on the way, he tried to put me down by saying things like, "You'll be in trouble if this proves to be a wild goose chase, lad."

Carl Whyler defended me, "And if he's right, he'll have stopped that bastard Dugal Whiston from getting the drop on us."

Once we reached Top Bay, Carl Whyler moved to the top of a large dune and began sweeping the waters with a set of night sights. Within seconds, Ed Fyfield's carping voice said, "Well, I can't see anyone in a boat. I told you this would be a waste of time."

"Well, I can see them," Whyler countered and loaded the rifles. He added, "It is Dugal Whiston and his gang as Bee Bee predicted; there are three boats out there, and the people in them are armed to the teeth. Whiston's not come here to say hello. I think you owe Bee Bee an apology."

Instead of saying anything, Ed Fyfield just glared at me. He'd been wrong, but he wasn't prepared to admit it.

Once Carl Whyler had loaded both rifles, he handed one to me and gave me a quick lesson on how to aim and fire even though I had already been on the ship's firing range. More importantly, I became conscious that all the people who had come with us were also preparing their guns for a fight.

Whyler whispered, "Pass it on. Don't start firing until the boats are about to beach."

After Whyler's instructions had gone around, everyone swivelled their guns towards the approaching danger.

I was reluctant to fire for a second or two because no one had fired at us, but then I heard Dugal Whiston call out, "Right. When we get ashore, I want to take as many prisoners as possible, and if anyone sees James Kinfrank, the kid they call Bee Bee, he's to be shot on sight. The Great One's orders."

Whyler gave me a nudge, "Why does he want to kill you?"

"Because of my dreams," I speculated. "I know too much."

While I was talking to Whyler, a rifle fired.

Because Whiston's boats were still two hundred metres from the beach, the single-shot warned them off. Realising they were moving into an ambush, two boats turned back. The occupants of the third boat suddenly started fighting, and a gun went off. Eventually, two men were tossed overboard, and the people remaining began rowing towards the shore, but I could hear them shouting, "Don't shoot, don't shoot."

Then confusion reigned because one of Whiston's boats came back to pick up the two men who'd been thrown overboard. Once the two men were rescued, Whiston's gang started firing, but it was apparent that they were firing at the third boat and not at us. In response, everyone in Whyler's group began firing back, forcing Whiston's boats to retreat again.

Eventually, the third boat beached, and the occupants ran towards us, hands raised. Once the fugitives were safe behind the dunes, Carl Whyler snapped, "Who fired too soon and scared them off?"

"I did," Ed Fyfield replied totally without remorse, "In case you have forgotten, I'm in charge around here, not you Carl, and you didn't ask for approval. I fired to scare them off because I wanted to avoid unnecessary bloodshed."

I didn't believe the excuse and concluded that Ed Fyfield had known all along that Whiston was on his way. He'd rubbished my report because he knew I was right; Whiston was about to invade. He'd fired his gun to foil Whyler's ambush.

As Ed Fyfield stalked away, Carl Whyler growled, "The man's an idiot!"

I was about to express my fears about Ed Fyfield's loyalty when Loud Mouth, the man who'd challenged Ed Fyfield's right to be leader, suddenly chirped up, "I don't know about you, but I think we need to have a new ballot. I've no confidence in Ed Fyfield anymore."

I was suddenly surprised when Akbar made his presence felt in my mind. Up until then, he'd usually come to me in dreams. Akbar supplied the truth, and I trotted out what he'd told me, "You can't trust Ed Fyfield. The Great Ones have influenced his judgment. Shortly, he will be totally under their control."

"Who are the Great Ones?" Whyler demanded.

"The same people who sent Whiston's gang to take us prisoner," I replied.

"So Ed Fyfield can't be trusted?" Whyler repeated.

"I'm afraid not," I said. "If you'd done nothing an hour ago; if you hadn't challenged Ed Fyfield's stance, Whiston's gang would have caught us by surprise and taken us all prisoner. Except me, of course, because the Great Ones want me dead."

"So where has Ed Fyfield gone?"

"Back to the camp, I think," someone said.

Whyler suddenly scrabbled in his pocket and pulled out a small device and began punching in a code. Noting the fevered activity, I said, "Is there something the matter?"

"I'm making sure that Ed Fyfield can't steal the shuttle," Whyler replied.

When the device bleeped, Whyler let out a sigh of relief and said, "Okay. We'll deal with Ed Fyfield when we catch up with him."

"You'd better make sure he hands over his Bowie sword first," I replied.

Whyler nodded, checked that the other two boats were not coming back and then talked to people who'd just come ashore. There were eight of them, four men and four women.

It swiftly became apparent that the fear of going back upriver had made them take the gamble and make their escape.

One of the women said, "They make us work for hours and then put us in filthy cages. Whiston said that unless we helped him capture the rest of you, our conditions would worsen."

One of the men added, "We had to help Whiston. They put our partners in the boat with us. They said if we'd disobeyed them, they said the two guards would shoot our partners."

After finishing talking to the escapees, Whyler came over to me and said, "Looks like they've had a bad time."

The comment immediately reminded me of the last dream that Akbar sent me. Without a doubt, the Great Ones were treating the survivors as enslaved people.

While I was still thinking, Whyler said, "So, what do we do now?"

I pointed to my hat, "We will have to make sure everyone wears hats like mine, or we're likely to be in serious trouble."

While we were still talking, one or two people stood up as if they intended to follow Ed Fyfield's lead and return to the camp. Whyler snapped, "Oy! Where are you going! Whiston's gang might come back."

He began to scan the river with the night sights again.

Picking up on another message from Akbar, I said, "Whiston's gang will try and land at Mid Bay and attack us from there."

Carl Whyler did not attempt to belittle my remark. Instead, he ordered everyone to move to Mid Bay.

By the time we arrived, Whiston's two boats were clearly visible. Following Whyler's command, we all spread out again and prepared to fire. I'd barely moved into position when Akbar shouted a mental warning, and I rolled over fast. A moment later, the sand where I'd been lying erupted.

While rolling over again, I caught a glimpse of Ed Fyfield standing behind me. A smile formed on his face as he swung the rifle towards me again. There was another report.

I'd expected to feel pain as a bullet ripped into my flesh. Instead, the evil smile on Ed Fyfields face evaporated, and he fell over. Glancing sideways, I realised the second shot had come from Whyler's rifle and in all probability, he'd save my life.

Someone moved towards Ed Fyfield, grabbed his rifle, checked his pulse and said, "He's still alive."

Because of the shooting, I'd half expected Whiston to give up on the attack, but his boats kept on moving towards Mid Bay. I then realised why the shots weren't heard. Unlike Top Bay, Mid Bay was rocky, and the breaking waves must have drowned out the sound of gunfire.

Noting that Whiston's boats were still moving towards the shore, Whyler whispered the same order he'd given on Top Bay, "Pass it on. Don't start firing until the boats are about to beach."

He'd barely issued the instruction before I saw a flurry of movement in my peripheral vision. I rolled sideways again just before Ed Fyfield launched himself at me. I saw the flash of a blade just before his Bowie sword slashed down at me and realised that he hadn't been completely disarmed.

Missing me, he raised his arm for another slash, but before he could stab me to death, there was another report from a gun, and a bullet ripped a hole in one of the arms of Ed Fyfield's tunic. I then saw Mary advancing with one of the handguns I'd acquired on the Empress.

Ed Fyfield swung towards her; Bowie sword raised but then changed his mind when he saw Mary's mask of hatred. Then, realising she would fire again, he threw himself over the crest of the sand dunes, rolled towards the pebble beach, raced towards the water, and then swam towards Whiston's boats.

I could tell that Carl Whyler wanted to tell everyone to open fire on him, but for some reason, he didn't. I watched as Ed Fyfield was pulled onto one of the boats; it turned away from the beach and disappeared into the night.

Mary came over and said, "Are you okay, Bee-Bee."

I nodded, "If it hadn't been for you and Carl, Ed Fyfield would have killed me."

While I was still contemplating my own mortality, Carl Whyler came over and said, "You're the oracle. What do we do now?"

Luckily for me, Akbar entered my mind again and gave me a solution, "The only safe landing beaches are Top Bay and this one. You'll have to leave two guards on each beach. Maximum four-hour shifts," I said, "We have to make sure Whiston can't sneak back, and if he does, the guards will sound the alarm."

Mary surprised me when she said, "Bee-Bee and I could take the first shift here if you like."

Whyler glanced at me and frowned, "Are you sure you're up to it?"

"Go and organise everyone else," I told him. "I'll be okay here with Mary."

Whyler handed me the night sights and said, "Make sure you stay alert."

As the rest moved away, I found a place in the dunes that gave a good view of the river but sheltered us from the wind's worst. After a long silence, Mary said, "Carl Whyler called you an oracle. What did he mean?"

After explaining my strange dreams, I told her that Suzanna Fyfield had been appointed the leader of the refugees and Dad her consort. Once I'd finished, Mary said, "When did you realise that Ed Fyfield was working for the Great Ones?"

"Not long ago," I replied. "I didn't really want to believe it, but now it's obvious Ed Fyfield and his sister are working for the Great Ones. Why else would Ed Fyfield try to help Whiston and then swim towards Whiston's people when he was found out?"

Chapter Ten

A New Day Dawns

Once we'd finished guard duty, Mary and I went back for breakfast. While we were eating, the horizon began to grow lighter. It was a relief that the long night had finished and that day returned.

We'd barely finished eating before Carl Whyler came over and said, "Okay, oracle, know anything about a missing programmer/controller?"

"Programmer/controller?"

Whyler held up the small box I'd seen him use to disable the shuttle. He said, "One like this one?"

When I shook my head, Whyler said, "Well, when you're doing your oracle thing, if you have any dreams about where it is, let me know. It's gone missing."

I said, "D'you think Ed Fyfield took it."

"It wouldn't do him much good if he had," Whyler replied dismissively, "It has a limited range."

Whyler added, "The only thing I can't understand is why Ed Fyfield didn't steal the shuttle while he had the chance."

Akbar whispered an answer again, and I repeated it word for word, "If Whiston's attack had come off, Ed Fyfield would have loaded it with all our possessions and then flown it up the valley to prove his loyalty to the Great Ones."

"Ah!" Whyler replied. He continued, "Back to business. Any ideas of what we do now?"

Pointing to my hat, I said, "Before we discuss anything. We need to kit everyone out with hats like these."

"Why?"

"Because the Great Ones will know what we're thinking otherwise," I replied.

Carl Whyler grabbed my cap and examined it closely, "How is this thing supposed to protect us?"

I just said, "Put it on."

Whyler did as instructed, even though his head was larger than mine. After putting my hat on and taking it off several times, he said, "Ever since we've landed, I've been getting a funny buzzing noise in my head. If I wear your hat, it disappears.

"That funny buzzing noise is the Great Ones listening in," I told him. "If you wear a hat covered in these beads, they can't read your mind so easily."

After trying the hat on several more times," Whyler said. "Where do you get these beads to go on the hats?"

Once I'd told him about the native bushes, Whyler rounded up a few people, and half an hour later, they returned with a massive pile of berries.

The group sat around the fire, piercing and roasting the berries and started attaching them to their hats.

When they'd finished, everyone agreed that the roasted berries were warding off the funny noises in their heads. Carl Whyler returned to his original question, "Right Bee Bee. Any ideas of what we do now? You seem to have all the answers."

I was tempted to remind Whyler of my age but decided against it; I was flattered that he took me seriously.

At that point, Akbar returned to my mind, so I followed his advice and said, "How much fuel is in the shuttle?"

"Enough for another trip to the Empress," Whyler replied. He qualified the statement. "As long as I think it's safe to do so."

"If we can go back," I said. "Can you find more fuel?"

Whyler shrugged, "I may be able to find more fuel, but that's in the lap of the Gods."

Akbar prompted me again, and I said, "I was thinking about moving somewhere else. Like a few hundred kilometres up the coast to an easily defensible position."

"Why d'you want to move?"

"Because Whiston's gang won't give up," I said. "We must leave these islands, or Whiston will surprise us one day and succeed in capturing everyone and killing me. Moving is the best option."

Whyler frowned, "What about the crops we've planted?"

"It will take some time for them to grow," I replied. "We can always come back and harvest the crops later."

"What if Whiston's gang move in and take over?"

Akbar prompted me again, "Believe me, it's unlikely the Great Ones will be interested in these islands. They just want us."

"What for?"

Akbar provided the answer again, "Slave labour and breeding purposes. They will allow us, humans, to multiply and work for them for a while. But once the Great Ones work out a way to create hybrids of us, of implanting their essence into human bodies, normal humans will become surplus to requirements."

"Hybrids?"

"That's how I interpret some of my dreams," I replied.

"So we move away from The Great Ones," Whyler said.

"The Fyfield Valley and the plateaux beyond is one great big prison," I replied. "The Great Ones can't get out, and they are only using Whiston and his gang because they can leave the Fyfield Valley. And Fyfield and Whiston only want to take the shuttle so they can raid the Empress for more supplies and ingratiate themselves with the Great Ones."

Whyler glanced at the shuttle, "Yeah! It's the jewel in the crown, always supposing the reports I'm awaiting deem the wreck safe enough to revisit."

Akbar prompted me again, "While were waiting for the reports, we could use the shuttle to find a new home. And then, if it is safe to do so, bring back as much as we can from the Empress. We could also catch some of the harmless millipedes or their eggs and breed them for food."

"Then what?"

"We abandon these islands," I replied. "Like I said, if we don't, Whiston will get lucky and take us by surprise one day."

Whyler began showing resistance, "So you want me to fly around using precious fuel looking for a new home?"

With Akbar still whispering in my ear, I countered, "I'm sure the shuttle will have flight recordings. So maybe we will find somewhere suitable using the shuttle's data and not waste fuel."

For the first time during the discussion, Whyler smiled, "Good thinking, Bee Bee."

~*~

The guards were kept on beach watch to ensure Whiston didn't sneak back, but I didn't join them. Instead, I spent hours in the shuttle with Whyler, checking and rechecking for suitable alternatives to the compass islands.

Eventually, we located large plateaux with a lake and a river that cascaded down the escarpment to water a forest below, but as it was only a hundred kilometres from the Compass Islands, I was unsure if it was suitable. On the spur of the moment, Whyler named it the new Lamington Plateau after the one on Earth.

After studying the steep rock walls surrounding the new Lamington Plateau and checking that they would make the area easily defensible. We then determined how much farmland would be available to us.

As there was plenty of ground on the plateaux, Whyler said, "So what do you think?"

As Akbar hadn't been in communication for several hours, I dodged the issue and said, "Let me think on it for a while."

After leaving the shuttle, I went to find Mary, who was on watch with Colin Pleach at Top Bay. I was pleased to note they were wearing their beaded hats. Joining them, I told them about the proposed move.

Colin said, "Why didn't you give it the go-ahead?"

"It's not up to me," I replied. "Everyone needs to be consulted."

He smiled, "Since Ed Fyfield did a runner, people have been talking. We all hate Dugal Whiston because he's a cold-blooded murderer. If it hadn't been for you, we'd all be his prisoners by now. Your visions saved them, and I'm sure they'd do anything you asked of them."

I immediately felt uncomfortable. Although Carl Whyler knew about my dreams because he'd been present when I spoke to Ed Fyfield, I hadn't realised that it was now common knowledge. So I said, "How do you know about my dreams?"

"Chas Foony told us," Colin Pleach said. "He also told us about your dream writing."

My face must have fallen because Colin added, "It wasn't a secret, was it?"

I mentally cursed. I was now the visionary, the reader of dreams. But what if Akbar told me to do something and it went wrong. The trust would evaporate in an instant.

Once Mary and Colin had been relieved of sentry duty, Colin went his own way and Mary and I went back to our tent, and I noticed that Chas's belongings weren't there.

When I queried the omission, Mary said, "He moved out this morning while you were in conference with Carl Whyler."

Mary added, "Now that Ed and Suzanne Fyfield have moved out. There are spare tents, and Chas thought it best if he moved into one of the other tents. He also said you were keeping him awake with all your sleep writing."

I was disappointed that Chas had decided to leave, but then I realised the real reason when Mary said, "I think it's best he left, Bee Bee. As you've just heard, he's been broadcasting our business to anyone who will listen. He's a gossip, and I don't like gossips."

I thought about what Colin Pleach had said, but before I could comment, Mary added, "He also told everyone that your Dad had run off with Suzanne Fyfield. I hadn't realised he'd told everyone until people started cold-shouldering me."

"Why would they do that?"

"I'm now the spare woman," Mary replied. "Some of the women are scared I'll try and run off with their partners."

She said, "I'm glad now that I didn't enter into a formal partnership contract with your Dad."

I frowned, "I thought you had a contract."

Mary shook her head, "Your Dad said it wasn't necessary, and I went along with it."

"But why are you glad?"

"Less hassle," she replied. "I don't need to dissolve anything."

I grimaced, "In case you've forgotten, we are marooned on an unknown planet and unlikely to be rescued. There is no one to dissolve anything."

She smiled at me, "That's true."

Then a slightly worried look formed on Mary's face, "You won't run out on me, will you? I've still got you, haven't I, Bee Bee?"

I nodded, "Of course you have. I promise I won't run off."

"Good," Mary replied and then said, "Can I ask you a favour?"

I nodded, "What is it?"

She said, "I don't want to be on my own with your Dad gone."

"I've told you," I replied. "I'm not going to run off."

She smiled, "I didn't mean that. D'you mind if I join you in here?

As Chas was unlikely to come back, I nodded, "Sure, as long as you are not going to go into hysterics when I start dream writing."

"I won't," she said and went through her bedroom area and collected her bedding. She laid out her bedclothes a discrete distance from mine.

~*~

While I was asleep, Akbar came to me again, and I told him about the proposal to transfer to the new Lamington

122

Plateau. He smiled, "That area is well away from the Great Ones and will be relatively safe."

"What d'you mean? Relatively safe?"

"The Great Ones will still send people after you, but if I were you, I'd locate any access points to the plateaux and defend them if you are wise," Akbar replied.

"But why would they still send people after us if we settle a long way away?"

"I can tell what they are thinking," Akbar replied. "They want your technology and to exploit you as slaves."

Mary stared at me as Chas had; she said, "You've been dream writing."

As always, I picked up my diary and glanced through it. I glanced up and said, "Have you read my diary?"

Mary shook her head, "I guessed you wouldn't want me to, but will you tell me about your dream?"

After telling her about the probable move to Lamington Plateau and the possibility that Whiston might still pursue us, Mary said, "Why would he?"

"He came to take us prisoner but instead lost eight hostages," I replied. "It won't make him popular with the Great Ones."

Chapter Eleven

The Millipede Hunt Starts

As Akbar suggested, we decided to capture some local millipedes to breed as farm animals. On the first day of the hunt, Carl Whyler sent me out with Colin Pleach, who'd been involved in millipede hunts before and knew how to find them.

At first, the conversation with Pleach was strained and stilted because of our previous discussions about my dreams, but I told Pleach that I hadn't been offended. From that moment onwards, his barriers lowered slightly. The semi-friendship increased with each juvenile giant millipede or batch of eggs we found.

As the hunt continued, Pleach eventually asked, "Why are we doing this?"

"The idea is that we'll take the juveniles and eggs back with us and breed them," I replied. "If we grow them on in pens, we don't have to continually hunt for them in inaccessible areas."

I added, "The other factor to consider is the ammunition we're using. Once it runs out, hunting won't be as easy as it is now."

Pleach nodded, "Suppose it makes sense. From what I've seen, the millipedes are quite happy to eat any vegetation going."

While locating more millipedes and bagging them, I started thinking about the Great Ones. Here we were attempting to farm the local fauna, and in the Fyfield Valley, the Great Ones were making plans to cultivate and enslave humanity.

Eventually, I pushed the thoughts out of my head because I couldn't deal with them

We were suddenly surprised by an Arcadian wolf. As it threw itself on Colin Pleach without any warning, it nearly succeeded in knocking him over. Luckily, Pleach's reflexes cut in, and he hit the wolf with the hatchet he was carrying. He hit it three or four times to finish it off.

We only realised why the beast had attacked without warning when we noticed that smaller grub like versions of the creature were emerging from an earth mound and realised that the adult had been trying to protect its offspring.

I thought about the grub that had nearly ended Whiston's life in the feeding chambers controlled by the Great Ones. From there, I considered Akbar's comments that the Great Ones had taken the original wildlife and had deliberately modified it.

After checking that there were no more adult wolves lurking in the underbrush, I glanced at the baby wolves.

I pulled out another sack and began pushing some baby wolves into it. Pleach shook his head in disbelief, "I thought we were supposed to be collecting young millipedes."

"We are," I replied, "But we may as well take these back too."

I pointed at the adult wolf that Pleach had killed, "When we go back, we'll take that with us. We need food, and if we're lucky, it'll taste okay."

We eventually tied a rope around the dead wolf and began dragging it home. While we were crunching our way through the undergrowth, Pleach said, "Any more news about going to New Lamington Plateau."

"Not yet. As I said before, it's just a proposal," I replied, "Nothing is set in stone."

"Didn't you say that Carl Whyler said he had reservations about the place?"

"Yes. And so do I," I replied.

"Why?"

"Our original idea had been to place as much distance between Whiston and ourselves as possible," I replied. "Somewhere further away from the Compass Islands and somewhere that Whiston would find hard to attack."

"But the plateaux isn't?"

"No," I said, "It's only a hundred kilometres from here."

"So why are you compromising?" Pleach replied almost accusingly.

"Because we can't waste shuttle fuel chasing all over the place looking for somewhere better," I said. "Most of the aerial photos we have in our possession show that most areas of New Australia are desert. The New Lamington Plateaux has water and vegetation. The only thing it appears to lack is animals which is one of the reasons for collecting millipedes."

"So it looks as if we will be forced to go to the New Lamington Plateau whether it's ideal or not."

I shrugged, "I don't know. All I do know is we can't stay here, and beggars can't be choosers."

Pleach then touched on a subject nearer home, "Heard from your father?"

"No," I replied, "And I don't expect to."

"Why not?"

Instead of revealing my dreams, I just shrugged, "I'm fairly sure he won't be back."

"Your mother must be devastated," Pleach speculated.

I was about to reveal that Mary was heartbroken, but Akbar suddenly intervened and somehow mind-linked me to Colin Pleach.

After only a few seconds of reading his mind, anger surged through me. Pleach was a predator, pure and simple. With Dad out of the way, he saw Mary as a possible conquest.

As more of Pleach's thoughts entered my mind, I was tempted to violence but controlled myself knowing that if I hit him, the rest of the group would just see me as a mindless aggressor. After all, they would not be able to see his intentions towards Mary as I could.

Akbar then sent me images of Pleach with other women. While my mind was still racing, a slight smile formed on Pleach's face, "I'll have to go and see your mother."

I reacted badly, "My mother's dead. Killed in a car crash years ago."

"I thought Mary was your mother?"

"No, she's not," I snapped, "And for your information, Mary's got me to look after her."

When Pleach smiled, as if unimpressed by my loyalty, I used the information that Akbar had supplied, "I saw you in a dream with other women. Maybe I should tell your life partner what I saw?"

When Pleach reddened, I added, "My dream was very explicit."

Enjoying his discomfort, I added, "Nothing left to the imagination."

Pleach glared at me and said, "You dare, and I'll make you regret it."

He stalked off, leaving me with the bags and the body of the Arcadian Wolf. As I was still angry, I didn't attempt to follow immediately.

Once he was well out of sight, I picked up the bags and began dragging the wolf again.

All went well until the wolf caught on a rock, and I had to go and investigate. It was then that I found the hatchet and rifle that Pleach had been carrying and noticed areas of shrub trampled underfoot. It was then I realised that Whiston was back, and he'd captured Pleach!

Chapter Twelve

Counterattack

After picking up Pleach's rifle, I dumped my load and began following the trampled brush. If it hadn't been for Akbar, I would have run headlong into a trap. His alert picked out two rear guards that Whiston had posted.

Some fields had simple windbreaks erected around them. I used them to screen my approach. Once I'd skirted around them, I set off towards our camp.

I then heard Whiston's voice, "Where is James Kinfrank, the kid they call Bee Bee."

Glancing up, I caught a glimpse of Colin Pleach and realised that Whiston must have discovered I'd been with Pleach before he was captured.

When Pleach didn't answer, Whiston struck him and screamed, "Where is James Kinfrank, the kid they call Bee Bee?"

Once Pleach had told Whiston, he sent five of his men to round me up. As the men went crashing through the underbrush, I did a headcount. Then, as I could only see four other men with Whiston, I decided to act.

Moving from behind the windbreaks because they provided little protection, I squirmed behind a large plastimetal container brought down by the shuttle but temporarily dumped in the open. I edged behind a low stone wall that someone had built from local rocks.

Feeling reasonably protected from possible return fire, I took careful aim and pulled the trigger.

Whiston let out a scream of pain and dived for cover. His henchmen began swinging their rifles around, but it was apparent that they hadn't worked out where I was because they started shooting at random. Knowing that Whiston would probably take hostages if I didn't act, I shot at the next man, and he went down. I took another one down.

Unable to locate my sniping position, Whiston's two remaining henchmen ran off

Knowing he was beaten, Whiston suddenly came out of cover and began zig-zag running to prevent me from getting another clear shot. He disappeared into the undergrowth.

Hearing shouts in the distance, I guessed that the five-man search party was on its way back, so I repositioned myself for another fight. By then, Carl Whyler and another man had picked up the rifles of the fallen and dived for cover too.

As the search party moved in on us, I levelled my rifle again, but I didn't have to fire another shot because Carl Whyler and the other man began pumping bullets at our adversaries.

Within seconds the battle was over, and Whiston's search party began running too. After calling out to Carl Whyler, I emerged from cover, briefly discussed the attack, and searched for Mary.

I found her hiding in a small wood together with several other people who'd been assigned to the fields.

They'd been lucky. Hearing the shouting from the camp, they realised that Whiston had returned and gone into hiding.

Once I'd taken Mary and the others back to the camp, we organised a hunt for Whiston and his men. After following tracks, we worked out the truth. Having been thwarted at the two bays, Whiston had bided his time and then returned. As the two bays were guarded, he'd found a way through the Mangrove entanglements, which we believed were impenetrable.

We were about to give up our search when a white flag began waving, and a man and a woman emerged from hiding. Their story was very similar to others who had deserted Whiston. The man had been Whiston's cannon fodder, and the woman was a hostage.

~*~

Once I was sure the raid was over, I went back with Carl Whyler and collected the bags of baby millipedes and the juvenile Arcadian wolves. While we were dragging back Pleach's kill, we heard a slight cracking in the underbrush. A moment later, Dugal Whiston emerged and fired his rifle at me.

I was immediately enveloped by the dark pyramid, and bony arms reached out to grab me.

Before I knew it, a bony hand had hold of me, and everything went dark.

Chapter Thirteen

Bee Bee, Can You Hear Me?

"Bee Bee, can you hear me?"

I could hear her, but somehow I couldn't answer. I then wondered where I was. After a while, I realised I was still in the dark pyramid, and the bony hand was still holding me fast.

"Bee Bee, can you hear me?"

Then, I heard Carl Whyler say, "I definitely saw him move."

"Bee Bee, can you hear me? Don't die on me, please."

I suddenly felt the bony hand release me, and then Akbar's face came into my mind. He was apologetic, "I'm sorry I left you for a while. My duties called me elsewhere."

"What happened?" I said.

Akbar reminded me of Dugal Whiston's murderous attack. He added, "But it will work out for the best."

"How d'you make that out?"

"Whiston managed to reach his boat that he'd hidden in the mangroves. He will return to the Great Ones and report that you are dead. Once they believe you are no longer a danger to them, they will take less interest in your people."

I suddenly felt very guilty. Because of my *gift,* I had brought down the wrath of the Great Ones on those around me."

Glancing around, I said, "Why am I still in the dark pyramid?"

"You should remain in the dark pyramid until you recover, Bee Bee," Akbar replied

"Bee Bee, can you hear me?"

I could hear her, but I still couldn't answer.

~*~

I don't know how long I remained in limbo inside the pyramid, but time seemed to stand still. Finally, after what seemed like an eternity, Akbar's dreamworld returned, and he sent me images of Dugan Whiston returning upriver. I was pleased to note that one of Whiston's arms was bandaged. It supplied proof that he'd been injured during the firefight.

As the boat crew paddled their way up the sluggish river, I caught a glimpse of Ed Fyfield. He was in the back of one of Whiston's boats, helping to paddle upstream.

The expression on his face spoke louder than a thousand words. Although he was strong enough to carry out the task, Fyfield obviously felt the role he'd been given beneath his dignity.

As Whiston's boat approached the short jetty that led to a small village, at least twenty Arcadian millipedes appeared, raced down the pier and occupied the landing point. Their demeanour indicated that they were intent on preventing Whiston from coming ashore.

I felt Whiston's surprise. He was expecting a hero's welcome because he thought he'd killed me; instead, his presence had been challenged.

While the stand-off continued, I noticed that Whiston and his men were wearing beaded hats similar to mine and concluded that Whiston must have learned the secret of blocking out the Great One's mind probing.

Akbar must have read my thoughts and confirmed them, "I have no doubt the other guardians passed this information to Whiston and his people."

I became annoyed, "Why are you talking to me and the other guardians talking to Whiston? Is this some sort of game you are playing?"

"I did not pass on the secret of the beaded hats," Akbar replied. "Not all your dreams come from me. You must have learnt about the beads from another guardian."

I thought about my dream about bead making and realised that Akbar was right. He was not the only guardian sending me messages.

"Why don't the other guardians declare themselves like you do," I demanded.

"They're under no obligation to do so," Akbar replied. "Most prefer to remain anonymous."

"Why?"

"Because acts of kindness carried out in good faith can be open to interpretation at a later date," Akbar replied.

"By remaining anonymous, they are evading future prosecution or condemnation."

"But I know your name."

"Don't be silly, Bee Bee," Akbar chided. "I don't have a name, as you well know. Akbar is a name of convenience."

When the boats still weren't allowed to land, I quizzed Akbar, and he gave me an insight into the situation, "The Great Ones communicate mainly through mind links. They have yet to fully understand your people or recognise many human individuals. At the moment, they can only see your people through millipede eyes. Arcadian millipedes have poor eyesight; they only latch onto noticeable differences between people, their size, shape and colouring."

I was immediately reminded of the millipede that came back with Carl Whyler on the shuttle. While it was trapped in the airlock, it seemed to follow my every movement.

More importantly, the mental threat it had sent me left me in little doubt that it had identified me.

Akbar picked up on my thoughts again and said, "The millipede in the airlock was following your thought patterns and your shape. You were easy to track because you weren't wearing a beaded hat."

He added, "I am expecting the millipedes on the jetty to issue a challenge to Whiston any minute now."

As if to confirm Akbar's comment, the Great Ones issued a mind message to Whiston, "Prove yourself. Tell us what you see on your identification."

I felt a sense of relief run through Whiston's system, and he put a hand in one pocket, produced a scrap of plastimetal paper and said, "I see a square, then a triangle followed by a circle ...."

As Whiston read out the lengthy pictogram code, I was reminded of the access codes that computer companies issued to ensure that their programs could only be used by paying subscribers.

Eventually, the millipedes pulled back, and Whiston was permitted to land.

Once the boats were tied up, Whiston took great delight in frog-marching Ed Fyfield to a holding cell with guns trained on him every inch of the way. Then, having ensured that Ed Fyfield couldn't escape, Whiston strode off with a group of henchmen surrounding him.

He entered a small side cave, an area designated by the Great Ones as a chapel., a place where humans could communicate with *Them* directly.

Once inside, Whiston stopped and bowed his head. A few seconds later, two light balls emerged from the sidewalls, and one said, "You have a report, Whiston?"

Whiston said, "Yes, Great Ones. I am pleased to inform you that the human called James Kinfrank or Bee Bee to his close acquaintances is dead. I shot him."

One of the light balls said, "Do you have proof of this?"

Whiston looked uncomfortable, "I do not have any physical evidence, but if you don't believe me, I will permit you to read my memories."

After doing his best to close down his active thoughts, Whiston removed his beaded hat, and the two light balls began hovering around his head. After a short while, they pulled back, and one said, "You have done well, Whiston. Your help with eliminating a dangerous enemy will not go unrewarded."

Whiston then added, "Ed Fyfield surrendered to me. I have placed him in a cell awaiting your instructions."

"Good work," the Great ones said, "We will interrogate him. Bring him to the interrogation cell."

Whiston looked alarmed, "You are going to interrogate him?"

Noting Whiston's concerns, the Great Ones said, "We are aware that there have been disagreements between you and Ed Fyfield in the past. This will not affect our judgement of you, Whiston. We make a point of interrogating everyone who comes here. It is our way."

Once the two light balls disappeared back into the walls, Whiston bowed to the Chapel walls again in case he was still under observation. Then, he replaced his beaded hat, picked up his guard, and went to Ed Fyfield's cell.

Once outside, Whiston kept away from the barred door, grinned at Fyfield and said, "Another one bites the dust."

Fyfield gave Whiston a hostile look, "And what does that mean?

"It means I've removed any possible opposition," Whiston gloated. "When I got here, your sister and Rob Kinfrank were living in the lap of luxury because the Great Ones had decided that they were the rulers of everyone on the Empress of Incognita. But that all changed when I

137

convinced them that Suzanne and Rob were unimportant. They are now locked up, and they placed me in charge. So now I have you in the bag; my position is secure."

Whiston clicked his fingers, and one of his guards came forward and handed him a stun pistol. Ed Fyfield reacted as anticipated and said, "Where did you get that?"

Whiston grinned. Waving the gun around, he said, "Obviously, you didn't know about these. And there was I thinking that you ship's officer types knew everything."

When Fyfield didn't react, Whiston said, "A large number of escape pods landed in this area. Some of the escape pods have stun guns in a special compartment. I only discovered that by chance."

He fired at Fyfield's left arm. Fyfield flinched and gave Whiston a baleful look, "What did you do that for?"

"Just making sure you don't try anything on," Whiston replied. He aimed at Fyfield's other arm and shot that too. He said, "Let him out."

As Ed Fyfield emerged, both arms hanging limply at his side, he said, "Where are you taking me?"

"To be interrogated by the Great Ones," Whiston replied.

When Fyfield didn't ask for any clarification, Whiston remembered his own interrogation and grinned, "It'll be interesting to see how tough you are when you're sent to the feeding chambers."

"What are the feeding chambers?"

The smile on Whiston's face widened, and he pushed his face close to Fyfield's, "You'll find out soon enough."

Whiston nodded to his men, and they began moving down a series of long winding tunnels to the interrogation chamber. Once they'd arrived, Whiston removed Ed Fyfield's beaded hat and tossed it to one side. Then, he ordered his men to strap Ed Fyfield onto an interrogation bench.

Once they'd finished, two light balls emerged from the sidewalls, and one dismissed Whiston and his men and waited until they were out of earshot.

Eventually, one of the light balls spoke to Ed Fyfield, "It would appear that your arms aren't working. Why is this?"

"Because Whiston shot me with a stun gun," Fyfield replied. He gave the fireball a challenging look. "Whiston told me that my sister and Rob Kinfrank have been locked up. That wasn't the deal. You said they'd be kept safe if I provided you with technical information."

Lightball One said, "What you have been told is untrue. Both Suzanne and Rob Kinfrank are being looked after properly."

"But Whiston said...."

"Forget Whiston! Whiston is a windbag and says a lot of things," Lightball One replied. "We tolerate his outbursts because he's a useful fool. He doesn't mind being disliked and most of your people fear him. He gets results because no one wants to cross him."

"So Whiston lied...."

"I told you to ignore what Whiston said." Lightball One cut in. "Both Suzanne and Rob Kinfrank are in congenial surroundings. You will be joining them shortly. Now back to Whiston. He has killed Bee Bee and brought you to us. So he has completed his main tasks other than capturing the shuttle. However, there are other tasks we could give him. We are allowing you the choice. You can allow him to remain as an enforcer or remove him."

"What exactly do you mean by 'remove him'?" Ed Fyfield asked.

"You could allow him to remain as an enforcer and let him continue in that role, or demote him, or we could have him eliminated. It depends on what value you place on his life," Lightball One replied.

Ed Fyfield's mind began to race and a slight smile formed on his lips. As Whiston had been arrogant and disrespectful during the up-river journey, had locked him in a cell when he'd arrived, and there had been bad blood between them in the past, Ed Fyfield had good reasons for disliking Whiston. Ordering the other man's death would have been sweet revenge, but Fyfield knew it would set a bad precedent and could rebound on him at a future date.

Detecting Fyfield's uncertainty, Lightball One said, "If you can tolerate his presence, we would prefer him to stay in his present role."

"So your suggestion is to let him live," Ed Fyfield replied.

"We wish for you to concentrate on our agreement," Lightball One replied, "Why not allow him to remain for the time being."

After thinking long and hard, Ed Fyfield nodded, "Very well. Let's go with your suggestion. Now can I see my sister?"

"We had hoped to discuss our agreement, but if you wish to ensure that we have kept our side of the bargain, further discussions can wait," Lightball One said.

Two millipedes immediately entered the room, tugged at the straps holding Fyfield down, and replaced his beaded hat.

Once he was free, Fyfield managed to struggle to his feet, and he followed the millipedes through a series of passages, climbing all the while.

Eventually, he felt cool external air and the smell of a wood-fired barbecue drifting in the wind. Once wholly outside, Fyfield saw a well-tended garden area surrounded by Arcadian moss ferns. On one side, there was also well-built living accommodation

close by. His sister was sitting around the barbecue with my Dad. After rushing over and embracing him, Suzanne said, "What's the matter with your arms?"

After explaining that Whiston had stunned them, Ed Fyfield did his best to sit down close to the barbecue. He said, "This may only be a fleeting visit. The Great Ones only let me come here to prove they'd honoured their side of the bargain, and I wanted to make sure you were being well looked after."

Ed Fyfield ran his eyes around the garden again and said, "How long have you been here?"

Suzanna said, "We were in the caves at first, but we were brought here a day or so ago."

"So no complaints?"

"No complaints," Suzanna replied. "Why is this only a fleeting visit?"

"Because the Great Ones haven't finished talking to me. There will be further discussions," Ed Fyfield replied.

As Fyfield slumped back, Dad looked worried, "Talking to you? What about? I was told the attacks on North Island went pear-shaped. Is that what they want to talk about?"

Ed Fyfield growled, "I've no idea what 'further discussions' will involve." He added, "Whiston made three attacks on North Island. They all failed. Worse, we didn't capture the shuttle."

Dad looked worried, "The Great Ones don't like failures."

"The failures can be laid at your son's door," Ed Fyfield growled. "That's why I was forced to swim out to Whiston's boat. Your son blew my cover. He used his mind-reading skills against Whiston and prepared a reception committee."

Dad looked peeved, "I've told you before. **Bee Bee is not my son**."

For a while, there was no sound other than the slight crackle of wood, and then Ed Fyfield coughed slightly, "Anyway, I know you say he's not your son, but this may be a body blow all the same."

Dad echoed, "Body blow?"

Ed Fyfield said, "I'm afraid I have some bad news for you, Rob."

"What bad news?"

"After the third attack, Dugan Whiston hid in the mangroves and laid in wait. You're son's dead. Dugan Whiston killed him. I saw Whiston take him down."

I'd expected Dad to show some emotion. Instead, he said, "I've already told you, Bee Bee is not my son. My wife wasn't averse to putting it about while we were on Mars. I had DNA tests carried out a few years after Bee Bee was born because I suspected he wasn't mine."

"And?"

Dad said, "He *wasn't* my son. He *was* a cuckoo."

The revelation shocked me, and so did the past tense that my Dad had used. He obviously didn't care that Dugal Whiston claimed to have killed me.

When silence greeted his acid comment, my Dad added, "My wife died in a car crash. along with her boyfriend, **Bee Bee's biological father**; Bee Bee survived the crash."

"How d'you know the boyfriend was Bee Bee's real father?"

"More DNA tests with the help of a private investigator," Dad replied.

"Sounds as if you were really peeved about discovering Bee Bee wasn't your real son," Ed Fyfield said.

"Wouldn't you be?" Dad snapped back.

"Sounds as if you wished he had died too," Ed Fyfield said.

I can't recall Dad's response because I was suddenly engulfed by my falling dream again, but everything suddenly made sense when I saw my father's laughing face.

The car crash might have been an accident, but I realised that Dad hadn't shed any tears when he heard about it.

I thought about the aftermath. When I'd survived, Dad had been forced to take me back and pretend to like me. But he couldn't manage to keep up the pretence. At that point, my thoughts became very dark. As Dad had been involved in terrorism, he would probably have learnt how to control a car remotely; what if Dad had engineered the car crash?

Perhaps he'd also hoped I'd die too.

I thought about the constant checks on what I was writing, and my thoughts became very dark. Could it have been that Dad had been scared that my memories of the accident would return, and I'd report my fears to the authorities?

By the time my falling dream had finished, Dad's conversation with Ed Fyfield had moved on, so I never did hear Dad's answer.

Reentering the conversation, I heard Dad say, "One thing I don't understand is what went wrong with the escape pods."

Not being a man who liked criticism, Ed Fyfield snapped, "What's that meant to mean?"

"Whoa," Dad cut in, "Whoa. I wasn't implying anything. What I meant was the pods scattered, and I don't understand why."

Ed Fyfield's pulled back from flash point and said, "I programmed my escape pod to land at the compass islands and linked to the others. I anticipated all the pods would land there too."

"So why didn't they?" Dad queried.

"I'm not sure, but I think some of my instructions were countermanded by the ships' auxiliary computer," Ed Fyfield replied. "I think it was spreading the risk."

"Spreading the risk?"

"Not putting all its eggs in one basket," Fyfield amplified. "If all the escape pods had landed in a problematic area, everyone could have died."

"But why did *you* choose to land in the Compass Islands and start planting crops?" Dad queried.

"Because I would have had to go to the Great Ones empty-handed," Ed Fyfield replied. "Until the shuttle arrived, I couldn't give them access to the Empress of Incognetta, or rather what was left of her. When Carl Whyler landed, I was tempted to fly back, but when Whyler showed me recordings of the exterior and interior, I changed my mind. The wreck is a death trap: one false move and its curtains. If Whyler wants to risk his life going there, it's his funeral. I'd rather stage another raid, take whatever supplies Whyler has brought back and capture the shuttle if possible."

Dad smiled, "Sounds like a plan."

It was at that point that two light balls appeared and said, "Now that you have seen your sister, it is time to continue our discussions."

The light balls led Ed Fyfield back to the interrogation room. However, Ed was offered a chair this time instead of being strapped down.

Lightball One said, "The survivors not under our joint control are becoming a problem. So I need you to take them prisoner and capture the shuttle."

I thought Whiston was dealing with that," Ed Fyfield said.

"Whiston failed, so we wish you to take over," Lightball One said.

"So you want me to organise a way of taking the islands and capturing the shuttle," Ed Fyfield replied.

"Things have moved on," Lightball One said. "The killing of the one they called Bee Bee must have spooked the survivors not under our joint control because we believe they have moved to a place they are calling the New Lamington Plateau."

Lightball One then provided Ed Fyfield with images of the plateaux and said, "We appreciate that taking this area will not be easy, but we will provide you will all assistance possible. Are you willing to take the task?"

Ed Fyfield nodded, "Of course."

"Good," Lightball One replied, "One other point. This is entirely your baby. We don't wish to involve Whiston in this operation."

Ed Fyfield smiled, "No, Whiston involved. That suits me."

146

"Bee Bee, can you hear me?"

This time I managed to speak, "Hi, Mary. Are you okay?"

Although I couldn't see Mary, I felt her grip my hand. Then the dark pyramid released me a moment later, and my eyes opened.

Mary immediately grabbed me and kissed me.

As my eyesight seemed fuzzy, I said, "Where am I?"

"You're in the shuttle," Mary replied. "They've hooked you up to the medical equipment in here."

Glancing sideways, I ran my eyes over the blurred outlines of some of the equipment and then said, "So what's wrong with me?"

"Don't you remember?"

Recalling what Akbar had told me, I said, "I know that Dugal Whiston ambushed me and shot me, but I don't remember anything else."

Carl Whyler's voice cut in, "Whiston fired twice, Bee Bee. The first bullet hit you with a glancing blow to the head. A few centimetres the other way, you'd be dead for sure. The second hit you in the chest."

He let out a slight chortle, "But you've come through it. You must be the luckiest kid alive. You got away with a concussion, heavy bruising and a few broken ribs."

"A few broken ribs?"

Carl Whyler said, "The second bullet hit this."

Unable to see, I said, "What's *this*?"

147

Moving towards me, Whyler handed me my diary. Whiston's bullet was still embedded in it. As I ran my fingers over it, Whyler said, "Good job, your diary was hardback and very thick. If it had been any thinner, the bullet would probably have gone through it and killed you."

Although Akbar's dream had provided most of the information, I still asked, "What happened to Whiston?"

"He escaped," Whyler replied, "I was more concerned about saving your life than chasing Whiston through the mangroves. In any case, if I'd gone after him on my own, he would probably have plugged me too."

Despite what I'd just seen in my last dream, I said, "You do realise we have to leave the Compass Islands and go to the New Lamington Plateau as soon as we can."

Whyler let out a slight laugh, "We're already on the New Lamington Plateau. It took two shuttle trips, but we still have enough fuel to go back to the Empress."

He added, "We've been feeding you intravenously, but you must be hungry."

I was, and I was thirsty too. So once Mary had given me something to eat and drink, Whyler disconnected me from the drip and catheter that helped my recovery and said, "We'll have to move you now you've recovered."

Realising that Whyler needed to return to the Empress of Incognita, I let them help me out.

Although my vision was still blurred, I noticed that several people were busily engaged in building permanent buildings from local materials. I also caught the slight glint of solar panels on some roofs.

As Mary led me toward our tent, I was also amazed by the greenery surrounding me. Don't ask me what the plants and the trees were because no one had named them. However, I noted that some bushes seemed to be fruiting. As I saw someone picking the date like fruit from one tree, I concluded they must have been deemed safe to eat. Noting my observations, Whyler said, "I think we can say this was a good move. There's plenty of food and water here, and your millipedes and wolves are growing fast."

Thinking about Akbar's warnings, I said, "You must make sure that we know about and paths up to the plateau in case Ed Fyfield tries to attack."

"I've checked it out," Whyler assured me. "I flew right around the plateau and used laser scanning to pick out any gullies that could be used to climb up. He pointed at a partially constructed stone-built structure and said, "So stop worrying. There is only one possible access point, and we have already started to fortify it. As it's close to our new village, manning it will be easy."

Whyler pointed to some cages and said, "See—those are the millipedes and Arcadian wolves you bagged." Seeing how large they'd grown, I said, "How long have I been unconscious?"

Whyler just shrugged, "A good while."

He added, "It's a good job you caught millipedes and Arcadian wolves. Unfortunately, the only animals we've seen up here are Arcadian pterodactyls, and they don't taste very nice to eat."

Once in the tent allocated to Mary and me, I was exhausted. Just the short walk from the shuttle had sapped my strength. When I awoke, Mary was reading my diary. She'd obviously removed the bullet because it was lying on top of a small table.

I was slightly annoyed, "That's private."

"Sorry!"

After thrusting the small book back at me, she said, "Who's Akbar?"

"I don't know," I replied. "Akbar says he's a guardian, and he has to make sure the Great Ones don't escape. And don't ask me who the Great Ones are because I don't know that either. All I do know is that Ed and Suzanne Fyfield are in cahoots with them.

"Your Dad, Rob is as well."

I nodded.

Mary then turned bitter, "He's with her!"

"I know," I replied and then told her about the car crash sequence I'd seen in my dreams and how Dad had more or less disowned me.

Mary looked embarrassed and then said, "I'm sorry. I should have told you."

"Told me what?"

"That your father knew that you weren't his," Mary replied.

I thought about the comment for a while and said, "If you'd told me, I probably wouldn't have believed you."

"Why not?"

I shrugged, "Because I wouldn't. It's hard to believe that Dad hated me so much."

There was a long pause, and then I said, "Did Dad kill Mum? Did he make her car fall into the Valles Marineris? Did he want to kill me too?"

The colour drained from Mary's face, "He said it was a terrible accident."

"But you don't think it was?"

Mary shrugged, "I don't know."

She looked at me pleadingly, "You're not going to leave me too, are you?"

"Why would I do that?" I replied. "You are not responsible for what Dad did."

A look of relief formed on her face, "Promise you won't leave me. If you do, I'll be all on my own."

"Okay," I said, "I promise I won't."

~*~

I can't remember precisely when Pleach turned up, but Mary had left the tent to do something. Glancing in nervously, Pleach said, "So, how are you feeling, Bee Bee?"

Although I felt far from well, I went for the customary understatement and said, "Not so bad."

"Glad to hear it," Pleach replied. Then his tone became wheedling, "I hope you won't say anything to Marj."

Marj was his life partner.

"About what?"

Pleach's face relaxed slightly, "Don't suppose you remember much because you were shot."

"I remember most of what happened," I disillusioned him. "What are you worried about?"

"About seeing me with another woman in your dream," Pleach replied.

I shrugged, "We've already discussed that. You leave Mary alone, and I won't rock your boat."

"You mean that?"

"I'm not an arsehole like you," I snapped. "I keep my word."

He extended the hand of friendship, but I didn't take it. I just repeated, "You leave Mary alone, and I'll keep schtum."

As Pleach gave me one of his grateful half-smiles and left the tent, I suddenly felt like a hypocrite. I'd been lamenting my Dad's lies, and here I was covering up for the likes of Pleach.

Chapter Fourteen

Return to the Empress

I heard the shuttle take off and guessed that Carl Whyler had gone back to the wreck of the Empress of Incognita. For a second or two, I half wished I'd gone with him. But then, I changed my mind because reports from the Empress indicated that conditions were getting worse, day by day.

Whyler knew that some of the remaining bulkheads were on the point of failing; going back was hazardous in the extreme. And yet, Carl Whyler had decided to take the risk because the wreck contained a lot of valuable salvage.

I thought about my dreams again. Ed Fyfield had said the wreck was a death trap. The Void Monster might claim me if I went on the shuttle again. Hadn't I come close enough to death already?

While I was still thinking about the VM, Mary carried in a portable computer, swung the screen towards me, and said, "Carl thought you might like to see what the conditions are like on the Empress."

I swiftly realised that Whyler was wearing a headcam. I could also tell that Whyler was wearing a pressure suit. My conclusion was based upon the occasional reflected body images coming back.

As I watched, the true extent of the damage seemed worse than I'd imagined.

Suddenly Akbar hit my mind and gave me a stark warning, "The Great Ones will attempt to steal the shuttle once Carl Whyler has loaded it."

"How?"

"That I don't know, but you must warn your friend."

After telling Mary to contact Whyler and warn him of a possible hijack, it didn't lighten my mood, and a deep sense of foreboding swept over me. Although I had only known Carl Whyler a short time, he was the sort of man I would have wanted as a father and not the one I had. But, more importantly, I feared losing Carl.

But I couldn't do anything. All I could do was watch as Whyler had rounded up the ship's droids and instructed them to start emptying surrounding storerooms and taking the contents to the shuttle's hold. Whyler opened a few more arms lockers and told the droids to load those too.

After watching for the best part of an hour, I began to relax. Maybe Akbar had been wrong for once. That was why the claxon sounding hit me with so much force. A moment later, I saw a sign flash up, "Shuttle launch procedure commenced."

The images coming from Whyler's headcam began jolting around. Then the screen in front of me blanked out. Akbar had been right; the Great Ones had stolen the shuttle and left Whyler trapped on the wreck.

Panicking, I tried to contact Akbar, but he didn't link.

I began thinking about what would happen to Whyler if he was forced to stay in the wreck. Although there would still be supplies to live on, he'd die a slow lingering death unless the bulkheads finally gave way and terminated his life.

Then, I began to think about another scenario. If the Great Ones had captured the shuttle once they'd unloaded all the stores that Whyler had loaded, there was a strong chance that they'd use the spacecraft to attack us again.

With this in mind, I staggered out of my tent and found myself in a dense fog. I later discovered that the plateaux and the forests below were often shrouded in fog until Salus, the system star, rose in the sky and drove it off.

After calling everyone together, I voiced my worries.

We were about to start dragging heavy items onto the landing area to prevent a landing when we heard the shuttle descending through the fog.

Everyone grabbed their guns and then waited for either Ed Fyfield or Whiston and his gang to pour out. Instead, a crackling voice boomed out, "What's going on?" and we realised that Whyler had returned.

Dropping our weapons, we all moved towards the shuttle. When Whyler emerged, he gave us a strange look, "Is something the matter?"

"You went off-air," I snapped. "We've been worried sick."

Whyler grinned, "Nice to know you care about me."

"What's been going on?"

After picking up a large log and jamming it in the door, he nodded at the shuttle, "Why don't we unload first."

~*~

It took us nearly an hour to unload and store all the equipment and food that Whyler had brought back. As some food production pods were still working, there was even some fresh food.

Once we'd finished and Whyler had eaten, I asked the obvious question, "So come on, spill. We saw the shuttle go into launch mode while you were still loading."

"You were right," Whyler said. "Someone did try to steal the shuttle, but your warning saved the day."

"How?"

Whyler produced his headcam and then let it run. I saw the alarm sign and heard the claxon startup. As the inner doors of the airlock began to close, one of the ship's droids moved into the gap, and the airlock door began bouncing against the obstruction.

After a while, the launch was aborted.

Whyler added his comments, "I heeded your warning and instructed the ship's droids to block the doors if the shuttle attempted to launch while I was not in it. Good job I did; I owe you one Bee Bee."

"But your transmissions stopped," I replied. "We were worried sick."

"I don't know why that happened either," Whyler admitted.

I then thought about the hours elapsed between the false launch and landing and quizzed Whyler about it.

Whyler said, "You remember we talked about a missing programmer/controller?"

"Yes," I replied.

"I suspect that Ed Fyfield is responsible for its disappearance," Whyler replied. "I also think he's programmed it so that the shuttle would go to him. So I spent the next hour searching for it."

"Did you find it?"

Whyler shook his head, "If it's on the shuttle, it's well hidden," Whyler replied.

"Well, we'll have to find it," I said.

Whyler gave me a rueful smile, produced the second programmer/controller, and began stripping it down. Inside was a small chip. He said, "Once the chip is programmed, it can be removed and easily hidden. It's a Trojan Horse. It doesn't take control of the shuttle until triggered."

"What triggers it?"

"I'm not sure, but when the airlock warning sounded, I'd just about filled every available space in the hold with salvaged items," Whyler replied. "Ed Fyfield doesn't just want the shuttle; he wants as much salvage as he can get his hands on."

Whyler's comments reminded me of the last dream Akbar had sent me of the human prisoners busily working in a sweatshop.

Whyler then put my thoughts into words, "Ed Fyfield wants to harvest as much technology as he can to ingratiate himself with his new masters."

"So, what are we going to do?"

"We're going to carry on as normal," Whyler replied. "I managed to refuel the shuttle, so I should be able to go back again a few times."

"You can't," I objected. "It's too dangerous."

Whyler shook his head, "I won't leave the shuttle on the next trip. Don't forget I've got droids to help me. I'll just control the loading from inside. If the Trojan Horse kicks in, I'll override it immediately."

"It'll still be risky," I objected.

Whyler said, "If we miss the opportunity to bring back what we can now, it will be an opportunity missed."

"Well, if you're going," I said. "I'm going with you."

Whyler shook his head, "No, you stay here."

"No," I insisted. "Last time the Trojan Horse cut off all links with you back here. If it hadn't been for the warning I sent you, you would have been trapped on the wreck."

Mary interrupted, "If you're going, I'm going too."

Whyler cursed under his breath.

Chapter Fifteen

Whyler Flies Again

After a great deal of argument, Whyler caved in, and Mary and I joined him in the shuttle. As we had plenty of fuel, I suggested we fly over the Compass Islands on the way up. Whyler agreed, but he made no attempt to linger. Instead, he took photographs to study later and then set off to the wreck.

Once in space, the silhouette of the wreck was picked out by the absence of stars. At first, it was just a massive join-the-dot image. But then, as our approach continued, the remains of the Empress of Incognita were suddenly illuminated by Salus, the system star.

As more and more of the Empress of Incognita came into view, I heard Mary take a sharp intake of breath as she saw where the mines had done their evil work. It was then that her nerves kicked in, "D'you think it will be safe to go onboard?"

"As I said, no one is leaving the shuttle," Whyler replied and then began manoeuvring towards an air-lock.

I queried the approach, "Is this the correct air-lock?"

"It's not the one we escaped from," Whyler replied. "As we have exhausted most of the salvage from Landing Bay 12, I have moved our operations to LB 23."

Twenty minutes later, the shuttle entered LB 23, but Whyler did not attempt to leave the shuttle. Instead, he activated the droids in LB 23 and used one of them to inspect the stores.

The droids began moving the stock into the shuttle's cargo hold. All seemed to be going well until Whyler let out a curse and began recalling all the droids.

Within seconds of the last machine making its way into LB 23 with their loads of salvage, one of the bulked shutters slammed down. Whyler went into an emergency abort, and the shuttle was ejected back into space.

As he regained control of the shuttle, Whyler said, "It was a good job we didn't get out."

Mary said, "Why, what happened?"

"I'm not sure," Whyler admitted, "There was a sudden depressurisation. Maybe a bulkhead failed."

"Are we going back to Arcadia?" I asked.

Whyler shook his head and said, "We're here, and we've used fuel to get here. We can't afford to waste valuable fuel."

He gave both Mary and me a stern look, "I warned you this would be dangerous."

He instructed the shuttle to move to the other side of the wreck. Once again, I was gripped with horror. Whyler put my thoughts into words, "It looks like the portside took a few heavy hits."

As the shuttle continued to creep forward, dodging trailing cables and mangled hull, Whyler said, "Not many people escaped from this side."

"How d'you know?"

"Very few of the escape pods have been launched," Whyler replied. "It's possible that the mines caused so much damage that there was no escape route to get to the pods."

He pointed towards an area that was very badly damaged, "The Empress's other shuttle would have been docked in there. We're lucky that this one survived."

The comment took me back to our escape from Rotunda 5. None of the escape pods had been available in that area. If our shuttle had been damaged, we would still be trapped in the wreck.

Eventually, the shuttle came alongside an undamaged loading bay, and Whyler instigated the docking sequence again. Within seconds, lights came on, and the airlock activated. Once the airlock had been repressurised, Whyler called on droid support, but only two machines appeared.

Whyler said, "Only two of you? Where are the others."

The lead machine said, "There are only two of us left. The others are damaged."

When Whyler let out a tongue click of annoyance, I said, "Something the matter?"

"I should have brought the droids from the other bay with us. The two droids out there are model Cs. They usually take direction from more intelligent droids."

"You didn't get the chance, did you?" I reminded him." You had to make an emergency exit from the last bay."

I could tell that Whyler wanted to leave the shuttle and check that they really were only two functioning droids available, but he remained where he was and instructed the droids on the type of supplies required and told them to bring some of the stores to the airlock so that he could inspect them. One of the droids hitched a trolley and then moved away with the other accompanying it.

After a lapse of ten minutes, the two droids returned. Whyler let out a grunt of dissatisfaction, noting that most items didn't justify transportation. Once he'd sorted the wheat from the chaff, Whyler told the droids to place the approved items in the hold.

As Whyler continued to click his tongue in frustration, I said, "Is something the matter?"

"It will take forever loading if we leave it to these droids," Whyler growled.

"How about if I get out and see what I can find. I'll be able to tell the droids what we want."

Mary let out a cry of alarm, "No, you mustn't."

"You heard what Carl just said," I snapped. "If I don't go and sort them out, finding what we need will take forever."

After checking the temperature and the air quality in the loading bay, instead of refusing my offer, Whyler opened a cupboard, pulled out a powerful torch, a heavy duffle coat and a simple hooded breathing mask and said, "You'll need these."

After pulling on the additional layer of clothing and the mask, I let myself out via the shuttle's airlock and stepped into the loading bay.

The bravado I'd shown inside the shuttle swiftly disappeared; even though the wreck's surviving computer system was doing its best to condition the surrounding air, it wasn't successful.

As the cold was biting into me, I wasted no time, and I instructed the droids to take me to the stores and then began searching out items that would be of long term use.

As I began moving around, widening my quest, I entered one area in virtual darkness.

The shock waves that had run through the Empress when the mines had struck had brought down large sections of suspended ceiling and the light fittings. I clicked on the torch and indicated what I wanted to the two droids.

No doubt I would have continued my search, but the torch picked out a massive bulge in one of the bulkhead walls, and I realised just how dangerous the wreck had become. After running the torch over the bulge again, I decided I'd done enough and set off back to the shuttle.

Partway there, a siren sounded, and the airlock doors began to close. I was going to be left behind! Fear turned into panic.

Then the siren stopped, and the airlock doors opened again. Wasting no time, I reentered the shuttle.

Mary greeted me with, "Thank God you're back."

I pulled my mask off and said, "I presume the Trojan just tried to take you on a joyride."

Whyler nodded, "As I said before, I've tried to locate the Trojan, but...."

"... It's well hidden," I finished.

Whyler's tone became slightly acid, "If you can locate it, oracle, please do."

"I'm sure I couldn't do any better, "I assured him. "It's just a pain in the arse."

Mary cut in with, "Bee Bee, you shouldn't use words like that!"

Whyler laughed, "I can think of a lot worse."

When the droids returned with some of the items I'd selected, Whyler smiled and said, "That's more like it."

We just waited while the two droids collected the stores I'd selected and loaded them onto the shuttle from that point onwards.

Once they'd finished, Whyler brought the shuttle out. But instead of heading back to New Lamington Plateau, Whyler made the shuttle move around the wreck again. When I raised a querying eyebrow, he said, "We may as well refuel if we can."

Once the shuttle was in the refuelling bay, the transfer was surprisingly fast, but Whyler seemed far from pleased.

When I questioned his demeanour, Whyler said, "Something is wrong with the fuel gauge."

He found an impact mark and added, "When Whiston fired at me, the bullet must have damaged it."

After interrogating the shuttle's computer, he let out a sigh of relief, "We have taken on more fuel, but that's it."

"That's it?"

Whyler said, "The tanks in this section are now empty. That's the last of the fuel unless we can find an undamaged dispenser."

"So, how many more trips to the wreck can we make on what you've just taken on board?"

Whyler made a computer calculation and said, "Two and a half."

"Two and a half?" Mary queried.

"It was meant as a joke," Whyler replied. "Once we return after this trip, we can make two more round trips, but a third one wouldn't make any sense. We could get here, but we wouldn't get back."

"So two more roundtrips, then?"

"Correct," Whyler replied. "Unless we can locate more fuel, but as I've interrogated the ship's computer and have already been told, all the tanks are either destroyed or empty, that's highly unlikely."

"Two more trips," Mary said.

Noting the fear in her voice, Whyler said, "There is no need for you to come."

He glanced at me, "You earned your corn today. Will you come back with me?"

Although going into the damaged hold had been a terrifying experience, I nodded, "Sure. It has to be done."

When we returned, we found the plateaux shrouded in mist again.

I'm pleased to say that down-shuttle went without incident, but Mary was not happy. She didn't want me to go back with Whyler because of the dangers. Our disagreement was put on hold when Whyler appeared with the photographs he'd taken over the Compass Islands.

At first, I couldn't understand why Whyler was getting so worked up. Then, he pointed out what concerned him, "Those are wooden huts, and they've been built on our old campsite."

He pointed out smoke in some areas. When Whyler zoomed in on various locations, I caught glimpses of upturned faces. When I frowned, Whyler said, "The reason you can see their faces is because, when I flew over the Compass Islands, everyone looked up."

He then added, "Anyone you recognise?"

Mary spoke first. Pointing to a face, she said, "That's Dugal Whiston."

While I was still staring at the photographs, Akbar entered my mind and said, "The Great Ones have decided to enlarge their territory by using some survivors as slave labour. If you examine your photographs, you will see that most people are shackled."

After checking the photographs in more detail, I concluded that Akbar was right. After bringing the issue to Whyler's attention, I said, "We will have to free them."

"And risk the shuttle?" Whyler challenged.

"The long night will return in a few hours," I reminded Whyler.

"I still don't like risking the shuttle," Whyler replied. "It will also use up a lot of fuel. If we try to rescue them, we may only have enough fuel for one more trip to the wreck."

"We have to rescue them," I said.

~*~

As I was tired after the flight to the wreck, I retired to bed despite it still being light. Mary joined me, but instead of letting me rest, she raised the issue of going back to the wreck. Despite Mary's worries, I must have fallen asleep because Akbar invaded my mind again. He sent me images of Ed and Suzanna Fyfield and my Dad inside one of the escape pods launched from the Empress of Incognita.

Glancing at my Dad, Ed Fyfield said, "Keep watch."

Dad went to the outer door and then began glancing around furtively. Eventually, Ed and Suzanna Fyfield stepped out. Ed Fyfield was holding something wrapped in a blanket. Once they were all back in one of the huts, Ed Fyfield removed the covering to reveal a strange-looking gun.

My Dad said, "What the hell's that?"

Ed Fyfield swung the gun in Dad's direction and pulled the trigger.

Dad flinched and then began running a hand down his left arm. Ed Fyfield smiled, "Does that answer your question?"

"It's a stun gun, right?"

"Give that man a gold star," Ed Fyfield replied, "This baby can cause a partial stun or a full stun. It can also spray large areas, knocking out whole groups in one go. The makers claim this gun will stop a charging elephant dead in its tracks. Not that there are elephants around here to test it on."

Dad rubbed his arm again and said, "Was it really necessary to do that? Use me for target practice!"

"I had to be sure the gun worked," Ed Fyfield said, grinning evilly

He added, "If we can get a few of these down to the Compass Island next time we go, we'll be ready for Whyler when he attempts to return with his mates."

"Why would Whyler return?"

"When the crops are grown, he will want to harvest them."

After a few seconds had elapsed, Fyfield added, "Let's also hope the stun guns are effective against Arcadian millipedes."

Suzanna said, "Why would you want to use them on the millipedes?"

Ed Fyfield gave her a sharp look, "Because we might need to."

"Why?"

"We may be the flavour of the month at the moment," Ed Fyfield said, "But once we have given the Great Ones what they want, they might turn on us. If we ever fall out with the Great Ones, we might need these."

After hiding the weapon under a floorboard, he said, "Right, let's go and collect a few more."

"A few more?"

"One in ten escape pods was equipped with one of these," Ed Fyfield revealed. "All we have to do is find them."

~*~

When I awoke, Mary's brow was wrinkled, "You did that dream writing thing again. I was talking to you one minute, and the next, you went into a trance and began scribbling away.

"I'm sorry about that," I replied. "I can't help it."

"When you start writing, it really gave me the creeps," Mary complained.

"I'm afraid you'll have to get used to it," I told her and then started, thinking about Ed Fyfield's new weapons.

If we went back to the Compass Islands and Ed Fyfield used them against us, we'd swiftly end up as his prisoners. With this in mind, I grabbed my diary, told Mary I had to see Carl Whyler and left the tent.

When I got there, Whyler's tent was firmly zipped up, and there was a DO NOT DISTURB sign pegged into the ground outside.

Someone saw me standing there and called out, "You'll have to come back later, Bee Bee."

I was on the point of retreating when the tent flap opened, and Whyler's head appeared. I also caught a glimpse of a woman in the background and vaguely recognised her. She was one of the women who'd escaped from Whiston and had come ashore at Top Bay.

Whyler said, "Did you want me?"

As Whyler made no attempt to let me in, I squatted cross-legged and talked to him via the tent flap.

"So, what's on your mind?" Whyler said. Pulling out my diary, I read out what I'd written down and said, "I think we should cancel going back to the Compass

Islands. If Ed Fyfield has these new guns, we could be running into real trouble."

Instead of agreeing, Whyler started cross-examining me.

Eventually, Whyler paraphrased what Ed Fyfield's dream time image had said, "Get a few of these down to the Compass Island next time we go, eh!"

"Yeah."

"Which means he hasn't taken them down there yet."

As I couldn't disagree with Whyler's interpretation, I said, "I suppose so."

Whyler grinned and said, "Let me show you something, Bee Bee," then his head disappeared from view. As it did, I obtained another clear view into his tent, but his woman had moved discreetly out of sight.

A few seconds later, the tent zip opened fully, and Whyler emerged partially dressed, holding one of the stun guns that I'd seen in my dreams and said, "Is that what you saw?"

When I nodded, Whyler added, "I was going to tell you, but you went to your tent with Mary. While we were away, one of our teams located a group of escape pods that landed on this plateaux."

"Some landed here?"

"They did,"

"Any survivors?"

Whyler shook his head, "The unknown virus killed them."

He then added, "I'd told the search team about the guns, and they have retrieved five, so rather than waiting until Ed Fyfield re-arms his men, why don't we wallop them while we have the initiative."

"Are we going to take the Compass Islands back?"

Whyler shook his head, "No. As we agreed before, that would be a waste of time. As Ed Fyfield lusts for power, he will keep attacking us if we go back. We should just rescue the enslaved people and then bring them back here. There is no point in attempting to go back permanently."

"But why is he lusting for power?"

Whyler shook his head, "That's a good question. Large parts of Earth were turned into deserts before most of humankind finally grew tired of war."

I began asking Whyler about things I had never been taught at school. As he told me about old battles and millions of people dying for the glory of Rome, deaths in trenches, thermonuclear explosions and biological warfare, I suddenly realised why the Mars community had outlawed many things. War was unspeakable; why speak of it if you don't have to?

I then began thinking about our proposed attack on the Compass Islands.

Whyler seemingly read my thoughts and said, "I am only proposing to go to the Compass Islands using minimum force. More importantly, we're going there to release people and not dominate them."

After agreeing with Whyler's sentiments, I said, "I still don't understand why Ed Fyfield is acting in the way he is?"

Whyler shrugged, "Probably because the disaster has released him from the straight-jacket of law. Like Dugal Whiston, there is nothing to restrain his psychopathic tendencies. With no police, army or law courts to worry about, it's very much, "Do as thy wilt is the whole of the law."

"So when will we fly back to the Compass Islands?"

"We?"

"I'm coming with you," I said. "Don't forget the Trojan Horse."

"Fair comment," Whyler replied. "Go and get some sleep. I'll come for you when I'm leaving."

When I returned to our tent, Mary started worrying again, but I told her I had to help Whyler free the enslaved people. This time she didn't say she wanted to come with me.

Chapter Sixteen

Return to the Compass Islands

Whyler came for me about four standard hours later. Although darkness had fallen, I could see that Whyler had fixed two of the stun guns to a set of mechanical arms that normally retracted into the shuttle.

Noting my observations, Whyler said, "I want to do this at minimum risk. I've rigged the guns so that they can be fired from inside the shuttle."

Once we set off, Whyler didn't head straight out to the coast. Instead, he flew towards one of the group of escape pods we'd seen when we'd first descended in the shuttle. Using the shuttles floodlights, we began searching the area. There were no signs of circling Arcadian pterodactyls this time, but grisly remains of human bodies were littered everywhere.

After checking for possible survivors and finding none, Whyler landed and gave me a set of override instructions if the Trojan Horse kicked in. Alarmed, I said, "Why are you going out there?"

"Because there are stun guns on some of these capsules, and I don't want Ed Fyfield acquiring them," Whyler replied. "And before you ask, I know which capsules have a gun and which ones don't."

As he was climbing out of the shuttle, Whyler took the added precaution of jamming the door with a log he'd thrown on board to prevent it from suddenly closing if the Trojan Horse activated. It was something he'd done ever since its evil presence had been discovered.

Before he left, he handed me a stun gun and said, "Watch my back."

I was half-tempted to make a joke because unless they'd become zombies, the skeleton's littered all around were not going to rise up against us.

Ten minutes later, Whyler returned with five stun guns slung from his shoulders. After dumping them, he began picking his way around other escape pods.

Once he'd returned with three more stun guns, he said, "Next site."

A few minutes later, Whyler landed at the next group of escape pods and repeated the operation. This time he only returned with four stun guns.

After going around several more sites and collecting a load more guns, Whyler said, "That's it," and removed the log from the door.

We took off again, headed back to the coast, and began crossing the open sea, with the floodlights picking out the rolling waves below.

Sensing a question on my lips, Whyler said, "I'm going to approach from the mangrove swamps because they are less likely to see us coming from that direction."

The comment reminded me of Whiston's last attack. Whiston had taken us by surprise by hacking his way through the jungle of mangroves. I consoled myself with the thought that at least we'd be flying over the Arcadian mangroves and not slashing our way through them.

A few minutes later, Whyler turned off the floodlights and just relied on the light coming from Arden, Arcadia's newly named moon. We then began our silent approach over the mangroves, using the photographs to locate the enslaved people.

Shortly afterwards, we saw at least twenty people working in the new fields by the light of primitive oil lamps. At the perimeter, there were three armed guards. One must have seen us because he raised his rifle. As Whyler anticipated some resistance, he was ready and took the guard out with one blast of the externally mounted stun guns. He also took down the other two guards for good measure and then landed.

The enslaved people close to the shuttle stared at us in disbelief. To break their trance, Whyler spoke through the external speakers, "Do you want to get away or not?"

Realising they were about to be rescued, they began hobbling towards the shuttle, hampered by the neck and leg chains that linked them together. Once by the door, they did their best to clamber onboard without injuring one another. Noting that the guards had been taken out, those higher up the field began the same hobbling run.

I realised that some enslaved people were dragging one of the guards behind them. Whyler made the shuttle move towards the group. He then left his seat, pointed at the guard and snapped, "So what's the story?"

"This guy is okay," Someone shouted out. "Don't leave him behind, please."

After nodding, Whyler frisked the guard and then told everyone to sit down as best they could. As the outer door shut and the shuttle took off, I noticed that none of the formerly enslaved people asked where they were going. They knew that it had to be a better place than where they'd been.

~*~

Once we'd landed and I'd helped Whyler remove the newcomers' shackles, I glanced at him and said, "So when are we going back to the wreck?"

Whyler gave me a sharp look, "Aren't you forgetting something?"

As Whyler didn't usually give me a hard time, I said, "Have I done something wrong?"

Whyler's demeanour changed slightly, "Didn't you notice the other fields and the other enslaved people working in them?"

When I shook my head, Whyler added, "Well, there were, and we can't leave a job half done."

Once, Whyler had ensured that the newcomers were being fed, he checked the stunned guard and said, "He's still alive."

Whyler ordered the guard to be chained up so he couldn't escape. He patted me on the shoulder, "Time to go back, Bee Bee."

Chapter Seventeen

Back to North Island Again

After take-off, Whyler took the shuttle out to sea again, and I anticipated he'd fly back over the mangroves once more, but I swiftly realised that wasn't his intention.

Sensing my unspoken questions, Whyler said, "A sensible pilot never retraces his course during a conflict. Ground forces might miss firing at you during the first fly by, but if you go back, they certainly will. They'll be ready for you."

He then gave me a history lesson, but I didn't really understand it because I'd never been taught Earth history. He said, "That's what happened to Baron von Richthofen. He was a fighter ace and had eighty kills to his record, but one day he doubled back, and a guy armed with a rifle started firing at him. Normally a rifle is not that good against a plane but a lucky bullet, or unlucky bullet if you were on his side, killed von Richthofen."

After turning back towards the Compass Islands, Whyler dropped low until the shuttle was nearly clipping the waves in the Fyfield River. He turned sharply inland.

A few seconds later, we saw billows of smoke. At first, I thought it was a typical burn, but then I saw flames leaping high into the sky and wondered what had happened. It was apparent the fire must have blazed out of control.

I thought Whyler had gone mad because instead of going around the smoke and flames, he headed straight towards it. I was tempted to challenge him, fearing that the shuttle could catch fire.

But then, as the shuttle burst out on the other side, I realised why Whyler had flown through the conflagration. As the shuttle was designed to withstand the heat of re-entry, it would not have caught fire. More importantly, he'd used the smoke and fire to screen his approach.

Moments later, we saw several groups of enslaved people and guards attempting to round them up. Whyler swiftly picked off the guards with the external guns and landed close to the first group of enslaved people.

From then on, it was virtually a re-run of what had happened a few hours before. The only exception, no one attempted to drag any of the guards with them this time.

Once we'd landed back on the plateau and had unshackled the prisoners, Whyler organised food and clothing and said, "Time to deal with outstanding matters."

I said, "Are we going back to the wreck?"

Whyler grinned, "Hold your horses."

He added, "There will be time enough for that but not at the moment. We've just increased our population by at least forty. So we will have to work out how to house them, feed them and find them something productive to do."

"You're not going to use them as slaves again, are you?"

Whyler gave me a sharp look, "Of course not, but they are going to have to work with everyone else to ensure our group survives."

We moved off and began making arrangements for one group of scavengers to return to the escape pods that had landed on the plateau and bring back the tents and any food supplies they could find. As the scavenging party set off, one formerly enslaved person came forward with a slightly crouched, subservient look on her face. She'd been freed but had still to shake off the mental scars of servitude.

She said, "Can I speak to you, please?"

When Whyler nodded, she said, "You're not going to punish Darren, are you?"

"Darren?"

The woman pointed towards the guard who'd been dragged onto the shuttle, "That's Darren. The others were brutal, but he let us have extra food when no one was watching."

Whyler said, "We'll take that into consideration. Thank you for telling us."

Once the woman had moved away and went back to tend to the captured guard, Whyler said, "Something else we need to do."

As we approached the chained man, the woman who'd spoken in his defence looked troubled. I wasn't really surprised.

Darren's body was convulsing, he was dribbling from his mouth, and the dark stains on his trousers indicated he'd also become incontinent.

Whyler said, "Don't look so worried. It's just the after-effects of being stunned. He'll soon recover."

The woman said, "Darren didn't want to be a guard, but they forced him."

"I'm sure he's got an excuse," Whyler replied, his tone edged with ice.

"They were going to feed him to the huge grubs if he didn't obey," the woman snapped back.

When Whyler didn't appear to believe her, I said, "She's probably telling the truth."

"How d'you know?"

"I'm the oracle, remember?" I replied. "I've seen this grub thing in my dreams. It's terrifying."

When Whyler seemed half-convinced, I added, "Why don't we give the woman some new clothes for Darren and let him recover. It will be no use trying to talk to him while he's still shaking."

Whyler nodded and went back to the main camp. During the short walk, I repeated a warning I'd given before, "I think we need to equip everyone who has joined us with beaded hats before we start talking to them. Otherwise, the Great Ones will listen in."

Whyler said, "Good thinking," and spoke to the woman I'd seen in his tent. After introducing her as Irada Glendrin, he asked her to organise a hat-making group. She'd barely disappeared when we heard the sound of raised voices and half expected to discover that a dispute had started between the ex-slaves and the established group. I then saw the foraging party returning, and they had five bedraggled people with them.

Whyler moved in and said, "Okay. So what's the story?"

One of the bedraggled, a man called Ullan Costra, said, "We came down in an escape pod with the others. We thought we were on our own. Everybody else died. We only survived because we ate salvavita."

Whyler frowned, "What's salvavita?"

Costra presented Whyler with an oddly shaped fruit and said, "That is a salvavita. We called it that because it saved our lives."

When Whyler's frown increased, Costra added, "Those who didn't eat salvavita died of the Arcadian plague. We ate the fruit and survived."

"It could just be a coincidence," Whyler said.

It was at that point that Akbar entered my mind again for the first time in hours and said, "If you are wise, you will find where the salvavita plants are growing and bring the seeds back and plant them."

Knowing that Whyler's scepticism was ill-founded, I spoke to Costra, "Can we keep this salvavita to study?"

When Costra nodded, I said, "We will need to find and cultivate these plants. Once you are settled, would you take us back so that we can collect seeds and bring them back here?"

Costra bowed and moved off, leaving, Whyler holding the fruit. A few seconds later, one of the other formerly enslaved people came over and asked, "Permission to speak?"

"Of course," Whyler replied.

"The Great Ones gave us fruit like that to eat, so we didn't die," the freeman said, "They didn't want us to die because we wouldn't be any use to them if we did."

~*~

As Whyler still showed a distinct reluctance to fly back to the wreck, I joined Ullan Costra and a group of scavengers going back to locate the salvavita plants. On the way, we all paused by the defence tower under construction

Glancing at Peter Fhahn, who'd been given the job of constructing it, I said, "So how's it going, Pete?"

"Slow," Fhahn admitted. "I've never done anything like this before. Not built a fort, that is."

Running my eyes over the mainly drystone structure so far built, I was amazed at the thickness of the walls. Fhahn presented me with a thumbnail sketch that Carl Whyler had given him, "Before he drew this, Carl Whyler managed to get some information from the computer on the Empress of Incognita. In olden times, all the fortifications had thick walls to stop them from being destroyed by catapults."

I was tempted to remind Fhahn that Ed Fyfield's people were unlikely to have massive catapults but let it slide. The tower was Carl Whyler's pigeon and not mine.

After running my eyes over the half-built structure, I saw one of Fhahn's helpers turning over an evil concoction, "What's that being mixed?"

"We're bedding some of the stones in mortar to strengthen the wall," Fhahn replied. "It's good stuff. Don't you remember, we built some stone walls on the Compass Islands."

The comment reminded me of the low stone wall I'd hidden behind while shooting at Whiston. When I nodded, Fhahn said, "That's why Carl Whyler gave me this job. He was impressed with my wall, so he told me to build this."

Eying the mortar again, I sniffed; it smelt vile.

Fhahn laughed, "We've grown used to the smell."

I said, "What's it made from?"

"We discovered the millipede and Arcadian wolf shells will turn into lime when cooked in a kiln," Fhahn replied. "It takes time and a lot of shells, but when the slaked lime is mixed with sand, it turns into a good mortar even though it stinks."

Running my eyes over the fortification again, I noticed there was no gate.

Fhahn said, "There's not supposed to be a gate. We don't want visitors unless they're invited. Anyone coming up the gully would face a solid wall at the top."

"Okay," I replied. "So, how does a visitor get in if they *were* invited?"

Fhahn waved me to the top of a timber scaffold and then pointed at a primitive lift suspended on salvaged plastimetal ropes. The hoisting platform came into view, loaded with heavy stones as I watched.

Fhahn explained, "There are loads of stones down below that have fallen off the cliff faces. Using them is a lot more sensible than quarrying the stone."

As Fhahn's helpers began unloading the stones, I noticed a sizeable handmade basket full of local fruits. Fhahn said, "Fruit trees grow in the wood below the New Lamington Plateau. Some of the women have gone down to pick them."

Realising the hoist was a weak link and might be used against us. I queried the security arrangements.

Fhahn said, "Don't worry. When the hoist's not in use, it is retracted and chained."

He then showed me the stout chains and heavy-duty padlocks, "When we're not here, we have to hand the keys over to Carl Whyler or someone deputised by him."

I have to confess I felt slightly miffed that Whyler hadn't included me as a keyholder but remembered that when I'd been shot, I hadn't recovered for some time. Having appointed a deputy key holder, why would Whyler change the arrangements?

I also thought about the women working below. What if they were taken hostage?

Fhahn pointed to an overhanging rock projecting over the forests below the New Lamington Plateau. As a woman was seated close to the edge, keeping lookout, I realised that Whyler had considered the issues.

I said, "That's good. Hopefully, Whiston will never attack us."

Fhahn shook his head, "It's Ed Fyfield you need to worry about; he *will* order an attack."

"You sound very sure of that."

"You're not the only one that gets dreams," Fhahn replied. "I get them sometimes; it's why I believe in what you say."

"What sort of dreams do you get?"

"They are difficult to explain," Fhahn said, "I see green caves with evil six-legged wolves like the ones you caught on North Island but much bigger, and I see our people being forced to manufacture things."

As our conversation continued, I remembered where I'd first met Peter Fhahn. He'd been one of the stewards who served us at the captain's table. I was reminded of one of Akbar's comments. He'd implied that I wasn't the only one with special mental skills. Presumably, Fhahn also had contacts with the guardians.

As my dreams about Ed Fyfield worried me, I asked, "So what do you know about Ed Fyfield?"

Fhahn shook his head as if he didn't want to remember. He said, "I knew Ed Fyfield when we were both in the militia."

After a slight pause, Fhahn added, "I've seen Ed Fyfield in action. They called him *The Butcher* because he killed so many people without any real cause. He's a psychopath, a real nasty piece of work."

Fhahn added, "Ed Fyfield is planning to invade this plateau, and he's capable of anything. He's seen an opportunity to build himself a kingdom on Arcadia, and that's what he's doing."

"A kingdom!"

Fhahn said, "Before democracy became fashionable most countries were run by ruthless men. They called themselves kings, princes, caesars, emperors and dictators. But the name didn't matter. They were all the same; really, they just chose different titles. People feared them and did as they were told. Believe me; Ed Fyfield wants to have power over all of us. Don't forget that he was prepared to enslave some of us. That surely speaks volumes."

Although I found Fhahn's beliefs slightly bizarre, I humoured him by not contradicting his assertions.

But then, as I broke away from Fhahn and followed Ullan Costra and the scavengers back into the forests, I began thinking about Fhahn's predictions. If Ed Fyfield intended to build his own empire, to become a King, *our* people could be in great danger.

After tramping through forests, Ullan Costra stopped and pointed the torch he'd been given at a group of fruiting bushes, "There they are, the salvavita plants."

Despite the darkness, everyone moved forward and began filling baskets. I noticed that one of the women was cutting off some branches, and I intervened.

I realised that the woman was Irada Glendrin. As she lived with Carl Whyler, I apologised and asked what she was doing. Glendrin said, "I used to work in the Empress's nurseries. They're for cuttings."

"Cuttings?"

"If I can root them," Glendrin replied. "It'll save a lot of time producing new plants."

When I frowned, Glendrin said, "It's obvious that you don't know much about horticulture."

After admitting that I didn't know very much about horticulture, Glendrin said, "I would suggest that everyone in the group learns how to grow things. We can no longer rely on factory farms."

After thinking about the land clearance and planting, I'd carried out on the Compass Islands; I realised she was right. Unfortunately, I didn't know much about anything. My head was stuffed with things that didn't prepare me for being marooned on Arcadia.

When we arrived back in camp loaded with the salvavita fruits, Carl Whyler homed in on Irada Glendrin, exchanged a couple of kisses and said, "Come on, I need your help."

"Are we going back to the wreck?"

"Forget the wreck for the time being I need you to help me with Darren, the guard we captured."

"Why?"

"You're the oracle," Whyler, "If he's lying, you will know."

Chapter Eighteen

Interrogating Darren

Darren had stopped shaking by the time we arrived. Whyler asked the woman who'd been looking after Darren to leave us for a while. Once She'd left us alone, Whyler said, "So do you want to go back and work for Dugal Whiston and Ed Fyfield?"

"Who is Ed Fyfield?" Darren replied. "I've never heard of him."

When I frowned, Whyler cut in, "Ed Fyfield has only just escaped, so maybe Darren has never met him."

Whyler revised his question, "So, do you want to go back and work for Dugal Whiston?"

Darren's answer was blunt, "No! I didn't want to work for him in the first place."

Carl Whyler immediately adopted the "bad cop" role, "So why did you?"

"Dugal Whiston threatened us all," Darren replied.

"How did he do that?"

"He took us to some caves," Darren replied. "And forced us to watch the wolf grubs being fed with live animals. Then, he said that if we disobeyed orders, they would drop us into the feeding chambers."

Akbar suddenly entered my mind and took the conversation off at a tangent. I said, "Describe these caves."

Darren shrugged, "They were caves, holes in the ground."

Akbar prompted me again, "Caves are dark. How did you see?"

Darren said, "It was easy to see in the caves. The walls and ceilings are covered with a green bioluminescent fungus."

As I'd seen the same thing during Akbar's dream visits, I played "good cop" and said, "Okay, I believe you."

With Akbar's prompting, I added, "Describe this grub you saw."

Darren said, "The grub was about two metres long. Its skin was mainly white, with brown blotches in places. It had six legs and big snapping jaws. After seeing it kill the animal thrown to it, I had nightmares for days afterwards. I kept on dreaming that I was thrown in."

Darren then glanced around and said, "I've heard talk that they are planning to attack this place and capture it."

"And how are they going to do that?" Whyler demanded.

Darren shrugged, "If I knew, I'd tell you. There was talk about the Great Ones loaning Dugal Whiston some of their millipede soldiers to spearhead the attack."

"You seem to know a lot for someone who didn't want to get involved," Whyler sniped.

Darren shrugged, "People talk. That's how we learn most things."

"So what you are telling us is just gossip," Whyler retorted.

"Call it what you want," Darren snapped back, "That's what I heard."

While Whyler was still grilling Darren, my mind began conjuring up images of the millipede that had died in the airlock. Not only were the millipedes the Great Ones had bred far larger than the ones we were eating, but they could also spit a toxic venom.

"So when are they going to attack us?" Whyler said.

Darren shrugged, "I'm not sure. Like I said, I've just heard whispers. Some people think that the idea has been shelved. Apparently, the millipedes can only survive for a day or so after leaving the Fyfield Valley."

"A day or so!" Whyler said. "Is that standard days or Arcadian days?"

Akbar made his presence felt again, "He is right; the millipedes will die very quickly, they will only survive one Arcadian day at the most once they leave the Fyfield Valley, but their deaths won't worry the Great Ones. They consider the millipedes to be expendable."

I said, "Why do the Great Ones want Dugal Whiston to attack us?"

"Because the Great Ones want everyone under their control," Darren replied. "They don't want a rival group of humans living on Arcadia and taking over the planet."

When Whyler shook his head in disbelief, Darren added, "Dugal Whiston has big plans; rumour has it he's done a deal with the Great Ones. He will be allowed to develop a human kingdom in the Lower Fyfield Valley. He will be king, of course."

Thinking about what Peter Fhahn had told me, I said, "Are you sure you've never heard of Ed Fyfield."

"Sure, I'm sure. I've never heard of him."

When I frowned, Whyler cut in, "Like I said, Ed Fyfield has only just escaped. So it's likely that Darren has never heard of him."

Whyler added, "If Dugal Whiston is allowed to set up a kingdom, what's in for the Great Ones?"

Darren raised his hands and wriggled his fingers around, "None of the creatures the Great Ones have enslaved have large brains and a means to make things with their hands. Humans do."

"There has to be more to it than that," Whyler replied.

"I do not doubt that Dugal Whiston will be expected to pay the Great Ones some tribute," Darren replied. "But I suspect he won't do that for long."

"How d'you mean?" Whyler queried.

Darren shrugged, "Dugal Whiston is not the sort of person who honours agreements for long."

I thought that the same would probably apply to Ed Fyfield. After discussing Dugal Whiston's ambitions to become Arcadia's first human overlord, Whyler went back to his original line of questioning as to when or how an attack would occur.

Unfortunately, the additional questioning proved unfruitful, but Whyler accepted that Darren would cause us no harm and undid his shackles.

At that point, Akbar entered my mind again and suggested we test our stun weapons on the captive millipedes and wolves in the pens. I said, "If they work on our animals, they will probably work against the Great Ones' animal army."

With this in mind, Whyler returned to his tent and came back with one of the stun guns. Then, we walked over to one of the millipede pens constructed out of a small ship's container with small air holes formed at various locations and opened one of the feeding hatches.

Anticipating more food, the millipedes began moving towards the hatch. Whyler fired his gun, and several of our millipedes stopped moving. As Whyler dropped the hatch, he let out a sigh of relief, "Thank God for that. The stun guns do work on millipedes."

I was slightly surprised, "Didn't you think our stun guns would work against them."

Whyler shrugged, "You saw the one that hid in the shuttle. It survived a trip in space. If it hadn't electrocuted itself, we might have been in serious trouble."

He turned to one of the people charged with feeding the millipedes, "Keep a check on them and let me know how long the stun effect lasts."

When the keeper nodded, Whyler moved away and went to check out the work on the tower. After discussing progress with Peter Fhahn, Whyler shook his head, "This is not going to be enough," and went back to the shuttle to interrogate the wreck's computer system. Eventually, he printed off a design and said, "That's what we need."

He showed it to me; I had never seen a timber fort before, so Whyler explained his ideas. Once he'd finished, he said, "I just hope we have enough time."

Chapter Nineteen

Building the Fort

After calling a meeting, Whyler explained that Dugal Whyler and Ed Fyfield might use giant Arcadian millipedes to attack the New Lamington Plateau. As the people in the shuttle bay had all seen a giant Arcadian millipede first-hand, Whyler didn't have much difficulty recruiting a labour force to build the fort. Fear was the driver.

Although a large area of land near the tower had been cleared for growing foodstuffs, Whyler wanted more land cleared for timber to build the fort.

As I joined the band, moving towards the spindly Arcadian eucalyptus trees further out, I started to doubt. It would take a lot of trees to build the structure that Whyler was proposing. Needing the wood, instead of burning, we tried using hand tools and were surprised by how challenging the stems were. Then someone remembered the two electric saws we'd brought back from the wreck. Luckily the same person had had the foresight to charge them from our solar arrays, and once we started to use the electric saws, progress improved considerably.

Once we'd chopped down the trees in the tower's vicinity, we then turned them into suitable palings.

While our group was on clearing detail, others had dug a deep trench and used the spoil to form an embankment. Once that was finished and consolidated, we used our palings, reinforced with stouter posts at centres, to build a tall palisade fence on top of the mound.

Once we'd finished, I walked around our new timber fort with Whyler, and I have to confess I was not that impressed with our handiwork. The sketch that Whyler had printed had indicated that the defence would be made from substantial logs. That had not been possible because the spindly trees we'd cut down weren't that thick. The structure we'd built wasn't really a fort; it was a fence on a mound.

Strangely, Whyler looked pleased. When I queried his optimism, he said, "The main danger from the millipedes is their poison. My guess is they can only spit venom for ten to fifteen metres. Our stun guns have an effective range of three hundred metres."

I was tempted to suggest that building the fort had been a waste of time, but Whyler said, "If the millipedes manage to get in close, our defences will provide us with some protection."

Whyler glanced around before deciding, "We need to clear more trees."

"Why?"

"The bigger the open area in front of the fort, the better range advantage we have," Whyler explained. With this in mind, Whyler ordered the clearance of more trees. He created several squads and let them practice firing the stun guns.

While the practice firing was still underway, Peter Fhahn came up with an idea and came back wearing one of the standard survival suits that had been packed away in the escape pods. Whyler gave Fhahn a beaming smile and acknowledged that the tough woven plastimetal fabric would probably be impervious to millipede venom.

With this in mind, Whyler began issuing survival suits to everyone. He also started a watch rota to ensure that the camp didn't fall victim to a surprise attack. As usual, Mary and I took one watch and placed ourselves in the partially completed stone-built defence tower.

We'd only taken up our positions when Peter Fhahn's voice floated up from below.

When I glanced down, Fhahn shouted up, "Whatever you do, don't shoot Muriel."

"Who's Muriel?"

"One of the Arcadian pterodactyls," Fhahn called back. "It injured a wing and was begging for food. Although Muriel's wing had repaired itself, she still comes back and begs. She's become very tame."

He climbed the scaffold and gave us a food bag, explaining, "Muriel likes fruit."

Thinking about the circling pterodactyls and the human skeletons I'd seen, I showed surprise, "Fruit?"

"Muriel won't touch meat," Fhahn replied. "It's the kind with the redhead that is carnivorous."

"So, what colour head has Muriel got?"

"Her head and body are brown, but she has white spots on her wings and tail," Fhahn said.

As Fhahn disappeared from view, I opened the bag and looked inside and found a mixture of chopped Arcadian dates, currents and salvavita seeds.

The rustling bag must have attracted her attention because Muriel landed close by. I then felt a slight mind jolt similar to when Akbar contacted me and realised that Muriel was also telepathic. After eyeing me cautiously, Muriel gave me a *feed me* prompt.

I threw her a sliced up Arcadian date, and she pounced on it. She transferred it to her wing fingers and began eating it with surprisingly dainty motions. Once Muriel had finished, she tossed the date skin away. As she was sitting close to the precipice, the skin fluttered down to the woodland below.

Some of the things that Irada Glendrin had taught me came flooding back to mind, and I vaguely wondered if the discarded skin still contained date seeds. If that was so, would date plants start growing down below?

While I was still thinking about plant reproduction, Muriel sent me another *feed me* message. This time I tried her on the salvavita seeds. Instead of attempting to eat them, Muriel gave them a look of contempt and back healed them into space.

As the seeds fluttered down, I began thinking about plant reproduction again. Still, the thought swiftly vanished when Muriel suddenly hopped forward, grabbed another date slice from the bag, and swiftly retreated.

Mary started laughing, "Crafty beggar isn't she?"

Once our shift was over, we cautioned the next duty watch not to harm Muriel and then returned to our tent. When we got there, I was surprised to find Muriel perched on the ridge of our tent. Then, I realised that Muriel had bonded with me because we both had mind skills.

Later on, I discovered befriending Muriel had some disadvantages because she must have let her colony know that humans were an easy touch when it came to food. Eventually, we had a group of at least twenty scrounging pterodactyls who'd joined her. When the group were hungry, they cackled like mad, and if something alarmed them, they let out high pitched screeches

As I'd become used to sleeping when I felt tired and not when day or night came upon me, I laid down. I must have fallen asleep because Akbar appeared in my mind within seconds and sent me images of Ed Fyfield and a group of men. As they were all wearing beaded hats similar to our people, I assumed the obvious. They had secrets they did not want to share with the Great Ones.

Ed Fyfield might have allied with the Great Ones, but he obviously didn't want them to know everything he was doing.

While I watched, one of the escape pods suddenly took off but didn't travel very far before it crash-landed again. A look of fury formed on Ed Fyfield's face, "If we had the shuttle, this would be easy."

Fearing Fyfield's anger, those around him offered no advice.

As Fyfield stalked off, Akbar's face appeared in my mind, and he said, "As you saw, Ed Fyfield is trying to relaunch the escape pods. He is hoping to use them against your plateaux."

Akbar then sent me images of escape pods loaded with Arcadian millipedes landing on New Lamington Plateaux and attacking our primitive fort. As the make-believe battle continued, one of Ed Fyfield's escape pods landed in the middle of our newly built defence, smashing down some of the walls.

A moment later, hundreds of millipedes emerged and swiftly overwhelmed our fort. I then saw myself trapped in one corner. A few minutes later, Ed Fyfield walked through the shattered defences, smirking all over his face.

As he walked toward me, he said, "So, we meet again, Bee Bee?"

I was surprised because I had assumed that Ed Fyfield thought I was dead. Fyfield pointed at the beaded hat I was wearing, "That may stop the Great Ones reading most of your thoughts, but some always seep through. They eventually realised that Dugal Whiston hadn't killed you."

When I didn't answer, Ed Fyfield half-turned, waved imperiously towards his cohorts, and when the man I'd called Dad all of my life stepped forward, Fyfield said, "You know what you have to do."

Rob Kinfrank, my former father, raised his gun and pointed it at me.

When he hesitated, Ed Fyfield said, "Come on, Rob, if you want my sister, you have a job to do."

Dad pulled the trigger, and the dark pyramid immediately engulfed me.

Out of the darkness, Akbar said, "If you don't want Ed Fyfield to win, you need to return to the wreck."

"Why?"

Akbar created an image of the wreck in response, but I didn't recognise it. When the view continued to move, I realised that I was observing a part of the wreck that had become obscured by damaged food production pods.

Akbar showed me images of two micro-fusers and a mobile force shield. "You will need these."

I pointed out the obvious, "Carl Whyler is showing a great deal of reluctance about returning to the wreck. It's now a death trap."

"He may be fearful," Akbar agreed. "but he needs to overcome his fears and do as I say."

"What if Ed Fyfield attacks while we are away?

Akbar said, "In my estimation, it will be at least two weeks before Ed Fyfield can work out how to reactivate and fly the escape pods. You will have to convince Carl Whyler to act now before it is too late."

~*~

When I came out of my dream state, Mary was staring at me, "You've been having those dreams again, haven't you?"

"I don't have much choice in the matter," I replied.

"So, what did you dream?"

I told her about the dream that Akbar had sent me, but I deliberately omitted to tell her about my visions of Dad shooting me in cold blood. After I'd finished, she said, "I don't want you to go back to the wreck. It's too dangerous."

Knowing that I had to do as instructed, I ignored her pleas and went to find Carl Whyler.

He did not receive my news well. When I told Whyler that we needed to go back to the wreck, Irada Glendrin had the same meltdown that Mary had had. Although I felt sorry for her, I was determined not to back down.

Eventually, Whyler suggested we go for a walk. Once away from Irada, I went into more detail about the visions I'd seen. When I'd finished, Whyler said, "I hope you realise that if your dreams hadn't proven to be right before, I'd be writing this off as an overactive imagination."

"But as you say, my dreams have proven correct before", I replied. "Don't forget if Whiston had managed to get ashore; we'd either be dead or working in a chain gang."

"Which is why I've taken your visions seriously," Whyler said.

Once we'd reached the fort, Whyler just stared at it. Eventually, he said, "So in your dream, an escape pod full of millipedes landed inside the fort."

"Yes," I replied. "We were overwhelmed in seconds."

After a lot more thought, Whyler said, "So you saw two micro-fusers and a mobile force shield in one of the Empress's holds."

When I said, "Yes," Whyler eventually said, "Okay, you win. We go back, but this will be the last flight."

Chapter Twenty

Our Final Trip to the Wreck

The last flight to the wreck proved to be pretty uneventful until we closed with it, and I had to remember the details from my dream. At first, my mind refused to cooperate, and I could feel my face going red because I feared that I'd let Whyler down.

But then, just as I'd finished kicking myself for the umpteenth time, I saw the damaged food production pods. Almost immediately, a massive image of Captain Wainwright was projected out into space, and his curt voice said, "There are people trapped in the suspension bays who need to be rescued."

Surprised at seeing Wainwight's image again, I said, "Thank God for that; the captain's still alive."

Whyler shook his head, "I suspect it's just a hologram. The ship's computer is probably just using it to make us more respectful of its wishes."

A partially obscured landing bay then lit up behind the debris of the mangled food production pods.

After manoeuvring the shuttle several times, a warning siren began sounding, and Whyler backed away, cursing. He said, "There may be people trapped there, but the approach is too risky. We could rip the shuttle open if we are not careful."

Captain Wainwright's message suddenly changed, "If the landing bay you have just tried is blocked, another bay is available."

A moment later, other lights came on, and Whyler began manoeuvring again. Finally, after nearly ten minutes, the unblocked bay became visible, and Whyler eased his way into it, and the airlock began to fill.

Captain Wainwright's projection returned and said, "The people who were trapped are being taken out of suspension and will be brought to the airlock within the next three hours."

Whyler went into echo mode, "Three hours? You are joking!"

Captain Wainwright's image responded, "You know as well as I do this process cannot be rushed, leading crewperson Whyler."

"How many are there to evacuate?"

"Fifteen," Wainwright replied.

I could tell that Whyler was worried. Finally, he put his thoughts into words, "Let's hope this airlock doesn't fail, or we may be trapped in here."

Although I shared Whyler's worries, I deliberately changed the subject. I said, "I thought we'd evacuated everyone. How come there are still people up here?"

"They probably couldn't get out, so the computer system kept them in suspension to keep them alive, hoping they would be rescued," Whyler replied. "It's an emergency procedure."

"But why weren't we told about these people before?" I asked.

Whyler just shrugged, "I've no idea. I presume that some of the auxiliary computer's systems are not talking to one another."

He began to mutter, "Three hours. That's all we need."

After a few moments of reflection, Whyler appeared to accept the situation, put his fears to one side and said, "Right! No unnecessary risks. We both stay here and let the droids do the work."

He contacted the ships' computer and asked for as many droids as it could spare. Once a few had appeared, Whyler let out a sigh, and I interpreted it as being one of relief.

The right type of droid had turned up. After explaining what was required, the droids set off on their mission and sent back video images. Although I was sitting in the comparative safety of the shuttle, my nose began reminding me of the foul air I'd experienced when I'd explored the wreck on my own.

I caught glimpses of the bulkheads. As many had bulges in them, I realised that they would eventually fail, and when they did, this part of the wreck would be rendered inaccessible without pressure suits. Finally, after what seemed like an eternity, the droids returned with the two micro-fusers and the mobile force shield and began loading them into the hold.

As soon as they'd finished, Whyler closed the hold doors, and I thought he was about to leave. But before I could express concern, Whyler contacted the wrecks computer and said, "How much longer before the fifteen people are ready for downshuttle?"

The computer was surprisingly upbeat, "The process has been expedited. The fifteen should be with you within the next twenty minutes."

Whyler then let out another sigh of relief and said, "Thank God for that."

As the clock ticked down, Whyler spoke to the ship's computer again to fill time. "Is Captain Wainwright still alive?"

There was a slight pause, and then the computer said, "I am afraid he's not."

Whyler asked after the other missing crew members, and the computer's reply was the same. I'm afraid they all died during the mine attack except for the Fyfields."

Whyler surprised me by saying, "Can we remove the holographic projector and take it with us?"

The computer considered the request and then consented. "The ship has no further use for it. You may take it."

There followed a flurry of droid activity as equipment was disconnected. Once the operation was complete, Whyler reopened the cargo bay and let the droids load the additional equipment.

As the loading continued, I asked the obvious question, "What do you want the hologram projector for?"

Whyler gave me an enigmatic smile, "Oh! I just thought it might come in useful."

Just as the loading was complete, I saw people in wheelchairs being propelled toward us by droids. Behind them, those that could walk struggled to keep up. The one thing they had in common was the expression on their faces; it said, "Please don't leave us behind."

I moved to the door and began helping them aboard. As the last group clambered aboard, I heard Whyler say, "Is that it?"

A few seconds later, the inner airlock began to close. Then, it suddenly opened again as two red-faced women triggered the release. I then heard their plaintive cry, "Don't go without us."

Whyler gave a sharp look., "Let them in, and then count everyone. We should have fifteen."

After doing as instructed, I made a quick headcount and called out, "We now have fifteen."

"Glad to hear it," Whyler replied.

He added, "You need to check and double-check in this game."

To reinforce the comment, Whyler made his own headcount and then instigated the launch procedure once more. Almost immediately, an alarm went off.

I glanced at one of the displays and realised that one of the droids had parked itself in the airlock, and the doors were bouncing off it. A sense of déjà vu gripped me. The scenario was the same as when Whyler had deliberately parked a droid in the airlock to prevent the shuttle from responding to the Trojan Horse.

The only difference was that the expletives from Whyler's lips indicated that this blockage was unexpected. Then the alarm stopped, and the ship's computer said, "I'm sorry to detain you, leading crewperson Whyler but we have discovered four more people in suspension."

"Discovered!?" Whyler snapped. "How could you have only just discovered them?"

"In case you have forgotten," the computer said. "This ship has been badly damaged. Some communication links are not functioning properly."

"Are you sure there are only four more?"

"Yes."

"And when will they get here?"

"In a few minutes," the computer replied.

As there was nothing Whyler could do, he made a short announcement even though the computer's conversation had been heard by everyone and sat there silently fuming.

The silence that gripped the shuttle was broken when a small voice piped up, "Why aren't we going, mummy?"

Embarrassed, the child's mother began explaining the situation in hushed tones. She'd barely finished when droids appeared with people in wheelchairs and headed for the airlock. As the approach continued, I did a headcount. There were six people and not four.

Whyler must have counted too because he growled, "That's all we need. A computer that can't add up."

As if realising its under-estimate, the ship's computer said, "The six additional people are now with you."

Whyler responded with, "We see them."

He dug the knife in, "You're not going to produce anymore, are you? We're taking more people than we should as it is."

208

"There are no more," the computer replied. It then added, "Now there are only bodies left."

Once the additional six people had climbed aboard, Whyler instigated the launch procedure again, and this time there was no attempt to prevent us from leaving.

After the airlock had depressurised, Whyler made the shuttle reverse at a snail's pace, checking each move to avoid the tangle of debris outside. But then, there was a nasty grating sound and the shuttle ground to a halt.

Mild panic started to run around the shuttle, but Whyler calmed it down by saying, "It's just a minor hitch. We'll soon be free."

I'm not sure if he really believed it, but his quiet comments dampened the panic.

He started an external inspection using the shuttle's external cameras and located a tangle of cable that had managed to snare the shuttle like a fisherman's net. After studying it for a few seconds, Whyler called the ship's computer again, "We're caught on some loose wiring. We need a maintenance droid."

My mind immediately took me back to my time when I'd just come out of suspension, and I'd seen fairies on the ceiling. There had been a maintenance droid outside then, but surely the mine strikes would have destroyed them all?

When Whylers's request went unanswered, I could feel the panic building up again. Then it subsided when the ship's computer said, "Two maintenance droids are on their way."

Two minutes later, one of the droids began inspecting the wires trapping the shuttle. Then there was a slight flare as it started cutting wires.

Someone called out, "Where's the second maintenance droid?"

Whyler answered by providing a second camera shot of another droid hacking away at the debris. Eventually, the two droids signalled for Whyler to move.

Once the shuttle was clear of the wreck, the two droids removed all the remaining wires. With the operation complete, Whyler continued to pull back and revealed just how badly damaged the Empress of Incognita really was.

Once again, I was appalled by the devastation wreaked by the mines. It was also apparent that the people on the shuttle felt the same way. One or two even started crying as they realised that the once-mighty Empress would no longer be able to transport them between the stars to Kepler-452.

After more manoeuvring, Whyler swung the shuttle around and set a course for the New Lamington Plateau. As the shuttle continued to descend, I glanced down and saw the Compass Islands and the snaking Fyfield River and realised that we were overflying Ed Fyfield's new domain.

I guessed the reason. Undoubtedly, Whyler would be taking photographs to assess Ed Fyfield's proposed invasion plans.

As we finally approached New Lamington Plateau, one of the two women, who'd nearly been left behind, gave me a prod and said, "Do you know if Irada Glendrin is okay?"

I nodded, "Yeah, she's with us."

I was tempted to ask how they knew Irada and how they'd become separated but let it pass because I'd never understood the complexities of the Empress of Incognita's suspension system.

As we finally landed, I felt a presence in my mind, and a small voice said, "Feed me".

When I climbed out, Mary came rushing toward me and embraced me. Then, she said, "Promise me you won't go back again."

Whyler cut in, "There's no chance of that. It's too dangerous to go back."

When Mary looked disbelieving, he added, "We wasted a lot of fuel moving between bays. There's probably enough fuel to reach the wreck but not enough to get back."

While we were still talking, Muriel landed on my shoulder and sent me another *feed me* message.

Whyler said, "You go. I'll get the others to sort out the new arrivals and empty the hold."

He added, "And don't forget to feed Muriel."

Surprised, I said, "How did you know she wanted food?

"You're not the only one that gets visions and hears things in the mind," Whyler replied. "That's why I believed you when you said Whiston would attack us."

I was about to ask questions, but Whyler said, "We'll talk another time. Now go and have some downtime."

Once we'd returned to our tent, I asked Mary for some food and fed Muriel. As the tiny pterodactyl took food from my hand, Mary squatted down beside me and said, "I think Muriel has been pining for you."

She added, "A bit like me. I was convinced you'd be killed going back to the wreck."

I was tempted to tell her how close we all came to death when we ran into the loose wires but decided against it. I was back safe, and so were many people who might have been forgotten.

She repeated, "I was convinced you'd be killed going back to the wreck."

"Well, I wasn't killed," I replied.

Mary moved in close, kissed me and said. "I'm so glad you weren't."

What happened next surprised me. Before I knew it, she took my hand and led me to her bed.

I thought about Dad and then scrubbed him from my mind. He wasn't my Dad. My real Dad was probably dead, killed by the jealously of the man I used to call Dad.

Chapter Twenty-One

Operation Redbeard

Akbar came to me again shortly after I slept, contentedly, next to Mary. This time he showed me images of one of Ed and Suzanna Fyfield and the man I'd called Dad working on the escape pods. One pod suddenly took off and travelled some distance before turning around and landing back at the take-off point again.

The smile on Ed Fyfield's face said it all. Unlike the last test, the pod had flown and very shortly, he'd be sending his forces against us. Fearful that an attack was imminent, I went to see Whyler and told him about my dream.

Whyler didn't seem at all surprised, and he said, "I know."

In explanation, he pulled out a tablet and began flicking through the photographs he'd taken. One glance was enough to establish that large numbers of people were working on the escape pods.

Then Whyler started a short video showing one of the escape pods rising from the ground and flying for the best part of five kilometres. The pod then turned around and landed back at Ed Fyfield's base. As it was very close to what Akbar had shown me in my dreams, it was proof that Ed Fyfield was still intent on mounting an attack on the New Lamington Plateau.

Whyler said, "I don't think it will be long before Ed Fyfield uses the escape pods against us. We have to get ready, and there is no time like the present."

As I followed Whyler to the machines that we'd recently reclaimed from the wreck, I heard chain saws at work and saw people busily clearing more trees and constructing open box-like structures with spikes on top.

Noting my observations, Whyler said, "I don't know how effective they will be, but if Ed Fyfield's re-conditioned escape pods have any control, the pilots will try to avoid our *hedgehogs* and will land in the free zone over there."

While we were still wheeling one of the micro-fusers into the fort, Darren, the ex-guard, came over and said, "You're expecting Ed Fyfield to attack us very shortly, aren't you?"

Whyler shrugged, "We are expecting him to attack, but we don't know when."

Darren held up a watch. The dial had the word *Redbeard* and numbers slowly ticking down.

Whyler gave Darren a sharp look, "Is this your watch?"

Darren shook his head, "One of the others stole it off one of the senior guards after you shot them. They gave it to me to say thank you for helping them."

"Okay," Whyler said, "What does it mean?"

Darren shrugged, "Dugal Whiston gave these watches to senior guards. Whiston liked to give code words for his operations. My guess is that Redbeard is his code word for an attack on you, but I don't know."

I said, "Whiston is no longer in charge anymore. Ed Fyfield is."

Whyler cut in, "Agreed, but he may have inherited Dugal Whiston's system." He glanced at the numbers ticking down, "If this is right, Ed Fyfield will attack in just over seven hours from now."

Darren intervened, "It could be a trick, of course."

"What makes you say that?" Whyler demanded.

Darren said, "Ed Fyfield probably knows that this watch has gone missing."

"Then why did you bring it to us?"

Darren shrugged, "I just reported it, that's all."

Akbar slid into my mind at that point and said, "There will be an attack. The guard who lost the watch never reported it missing."

"Why not?" I mentally demanded.

"Dugal Whiston and Ed Fyfield rule by fear," Akbar replied. "If you were the guard who'd lost a watch, would you tell either of them?"

Realising that Akbar was right, I intervened, "Thanks for letting us know, Darren. We'll take it from here. Thanks! Good man! You can go now."

As Darren thanked me and walked away minus the watch, Whyler became stroppy, "I hadn't finished with him. Why did you thank him? He said it could be a rouse."

"On the other hand, it might not be," I replied and then unashamedly plagued Akbar's word, "Dugal Whiston and Ed Fyfield rule by fear. They have the habit of shooting messengers bringing bad news. If you were the guard who'd lost a watch, would you tell either of them? Would you take the risk and give him the bad news?"

"So there will be an attack!"

"Undoubtedly," I replied. "So we need to get busy."

Chapter Twenty-Two

Preparing the Defences

Once the two micro-fusers had been placed inside the stone tower for safety, the mobile force shield was then placed next to them and wired together. After ensuring that the area was clear, Whyler flipped a switch and the force field formed over a wide area. I noted that Whyler had assured that the top of the stone tower was still projecting above the force shield.

As a final refinement, Whyler formed three doorways in the force shield. Two were facing onto the cleared area, and one gave access to the top of the tower. He flipped them open and shut them several times to ensure they worked correctly.

Satisfied with the end result, he took me up the tower, and I realised why he'd kept the force shield low. Having the tower projecting above the force shield meant that people in the building could fire down on any attackers.

I turned and glanced down at the forest far below. As I did so, Akbar sent me images of escape pods crashing short of the plateaux and hundreds of millipedes emerging and racing up the near-vertical cliff faces with an ease that shocked me.

Fearful, I said, "The cliffs might deter humans, but the millipedes will climb them, no problem. Anyone standing where we are will be very vulnerable."

Whyler considered my comments, and when we left the tower, he adjusted the force field to encapsulate the building. He created a window in front of the tower to allow defenders to fire down. Once he'd finished, he said, "Let's go back up."

Once back at the top, I was impressed by the change. With the shimmering force shield preventing an attack from the rear or above. I now felt safe. More importantly, the window gave an unimpeded view of the clearing.

Whyler gave me a slight, smile, "Problem solved?"

When I nodded, Whyler led me down again, walked out through one of the forces shield doorways, and strode off. I followed without thinking, caught him up and then said, "What are you up to now?"

"I'm going to make sure this force shield is as good as we hope it is."

He called in a group that had been practising with the stun guns and told them to fire at the force shield. When the four aimed and fired in unison, the force shield reacted by creating a rainbow of colour that rippled around it but didn't collapse.

Whyler instructed them to repeat the test at maximum power. The force shield visibly deformed this time but sprang back and then provided another rainbow display. After telling the group to return their guns to minimum power, Whyler dismissed them and then said, "I'm reasonably happy with that, but there is a lot more to do."

"Like what?"

"If that watch was right, they will attack us just after night has fallen," Whyler replied. "So I want every available lamp hitched up so that we can see what we've firing at. We also need to dismantle the tents and store them in the fort. If there's any room, we also need to bring in all our salvage so that Ed Fyfield can't get his hands on it."

I glanced towards the permanent houses that some people had begun to build but deliberately didn't point out the obvious. Although the new dwellings were further out, I suspected that most of them would be damaged if escape pods began swooping in on our village.

The next few hours were busy, but most urgent jobs were completed, and most people decided to day sleep to be ready for a long night battle. I was about to do just that when Whyler said, "One last thing."

"What's that?"

"Run towards the shuttle as if all the hounds in hell are chasing after you," he said.

"Eh! Why?"

"Don't ask questions. Just do it," Whyler growled and then took me just outside the fort. "Run from here to the shuttle and jump aboard."

Although mystified, I did as Whyler requested. In fact, I repeated the exercise four times before he was satisfied. He then said, "Right! Go and get some rest."

As our tent had been dismantled, Mary and I slept in the stone tower along with five or six other people. Conditions were cramped, to say the least. It was made all the worse because Muriel, our tame pterodactyl, had obviously picked up on our worries about the impending attack because she became agitated and kept on fluttering in and out.

Once I did manage to fall asleep, Akbar came into my mind, and I saw Dugal Whiston in deep conversation with another man.

Akbar picked up on my thoughts and said, "The other man is Xi Myi; he is one of Whiston's associates."

"I don't like it," Myi said. "If Ed Fyfield finds out, I'll be in real trouble."

"All I'm asking you to do is to get one of your people to swap places with me," Whiston replied. "We are similar build, and you've just told me that you'll all be wearing standard survival suits. If we swap, who will know?"

Myi wasn't convinced, "It's well known that you and Ed Fyfield hate one another's guts.

Whiston smiled, "Do you like working for Ed Fyfield? Weren't things better for you when I was in charge?"

Myi responded as Whiston had anticipated, "Of course, I'd rather work for you. Ed Fyfield's a slave driver."

"Good," Whiston replied. "That's settled."

Myi frowned, "What are you up to?"

"Let's just say Ed Fyfield won't be coming back."

When the first dream session ended, Akbar transported me closer to home, and I saw Whyler searching the shuttle's interior.

220

Although I suspected that Whyler was still trying to find the Trojan Horse that had attempted to hijack the shuttle on several occasions, I couldn't work out why he was wasting his time. As he'd told me several times that the shuttle was low on fuel, it didn't appear to be worth the effort.

After allowing me to watch Whyler checking and rechecking every nook and cranny on the shuttle, Akbar pulled me back to reality and said, "You must be wary. Fyfield may bring the attack forward."

Why?"

Akbar said, "Fyfield is an impatient and impulsive man. He may grow tired of waiting until dark."

Chapter Twenty-Three

Invasion

I awoke suddenly because Muriel and the other pterodactyls were all squawking like mad, and Muriel was sending me mind messages showing the images of several escape pods in flight.

Without querying the warning, I rushed towards the force shield and turned it on. I then turned on the lighting system even though it was still light outside.

Whyler appeared a few seconds later and tapped his watch, "It's not even turned dusk yet; what's going on?"

"I'm not sure," I replied, "Didn't you hear the pterodactyls squawking? Come on; we need to check outside."

I grabbed my gun and swiftly climbed the tower with Whyler close on my heels.

At the top, I found the man assigned to guard duty asleep at his post. Annoyed, Whyler clubbed him into wakefulness, turned to glance out and let out an oath. There were at least thirty escape pods flying towards us.

Without making further comment, Whyler rushed back down, closed the two doors in the force shield and then began hitting a gong. Once he was satisfied that he'd roused everyone, he came back up the tower to join me.

I realised that Akbar's prediction had come true as it was still light. Fyfield had decided to bring the attack forward by several hours. I changed my mind about the Redbeard message on the watch may have been a deliberate ploy. Realising that one of the watches was missing and had tried to feed us misinformation.

A few seconds later, the first escape pod came hurtling towards us, and as Akbar had predicted, it came crashing down on the fort. As the force shield gave under the pod's weight, I expected it to burst through, but then the shield resisted, and the missile flew off into the clearing and split open when it landed on one of Whyler's *hedgehogs*. When millipedes began streaming out, I started blasting them.

A moment later, another pod hit the force shield, and there was a repetition. The dome bulged in alarmingly but resisted; the pod bounced off, and Arcadian millipedes began racing towards the fort.

As minimum stun had little effect, Whyler and I switched to kill mode and began knocking them down, but the batteries were drained within seconds. Whyler responded by grabbing the sleepy guard's gun and snapped, "Make yourself useful and bring us fully charged guns."

Wanting to make amends, Sleepy shot downstairs and returned with three replacement guns. As soon as he came back, I grabbed one and rejoined Whyler pumping shots into the millipedes.

Suddenly the force shield buckled, and rainbow colours went surging around it. As I'd seen Whyler deliberately shooting at the force dome, I knew what was causing the ripples of colour. Ed Fyfield's people were intentionally blasting the shield with combined fire in the hope of making it collapse.

While the ripples were still surging around the force shield, a mass of millipedes moved towards us in a wave. Directly behind them were carts with large shields mounted on the front to protect the human assailants behind.

Whyler dropped his stun weapon and picked up his rifle. After he'd pumped half a dozen bullets into the shields, we were rewarded by screams of pain and the sight of human figures running back to the safety of the woods. They began firing at us and the force shield again.

As power blasts were now aimed at our position, Whyler gave me a nudge and went down the stairs. I stooped low and followed him. He closed the upper window and formed several slit windows that allowed people to fire off the mound behind the fence but were narrow enough to keep the millipedes out.

With six gunners instead of just two, very soon, the piles of millipedes littering the ground outside swiftly grew.

As the assault finally petered out, Whyler closed half of the lower windows to prevent too many stray shots from being fired into the power dome and partially opened the one on the tower again. We began viewing the carnage outside when we were back in the building. As there were now hundreds of dead millipedes strewn across the clearing, it was apparent that we'd already destroyed a large part of Whyler's animal army.

After a lull of twenty minutes, more stun shots began hitting the force shield again. I was pleased to note that return shots were being fired from the people handling the lower windows.

But as the incoming shots increased in volume, I could sense that the protective dome was getting close to collapsing again. Whyler responded by pumping return shots into the tree line and shouting for everyone to follow suit.

As the fire and return fire continued, the force shield visibly buckled, and shouts of alarm began drifting up from below. The cries became worse as the shield finally collapsed completely.

Within seconds, the millipedes began moving towards us again, and everyone began blasting at them. When they came within twenty metres of the barrier, waves of panic swept over me as I envisaged becoming engaged in a face to face encounter with the evil-looking creatures.

Then, just as it looked as if the fort would be overwhelmed, the force shield suddenly reactivated. Undeterred, the millipedes kept on moving toward us.

Whyler told me to carry on firing and then rushed down the stairs to close the lower windows, but he needn't have worried because as soon as the millipedes began climbing onto the force shield, they started bursting into flames.

As I was still in position in the upper tower window, I could hear the shrieks of pain as they began dying en mass. Eventually, the millipede attack faltered, and some survivors started moving back towards cover. Others just stayed where they were, alive but not quite dead.

As I continued to stare down, Akbar whispered, "The millipedes have been away from their natural home for too long. They are starting to die."

I said, "So once all the millipedes have died, presumably, Ed Fyfield and his people will be on their own."

"Don't underestimate him," Akbar cautioned. "He'll realise that he's trapped and will fight much harder."

While I still thought-talked to Akbar, I heard rifle fire followed by a distinct ping. There were then several more shots in swift succession. As more pings rang out, I realised that someone was shooting at the floodlighting. Catching sight of the gunman, I fired back and saw him drop. Only then did I realise that I'd left my stun gun on max.

I don't know if it was my unintentional killing, but everything went very quiet, and I found the lull in the fighting worse than flying bullets. After a while, vague whispered conversations started up from below. Then I heard a clumping on the stairs, and Whyler returned with four recharged stun guns and a cup of *ersatz* tea that someone had brewed up from the dried salvavita leaves. It tasted disgusting, but I still drank it.

After taking up a position where he could see out but was unlikely to be shot, Whyler confirmed my thoughts, "This is the worst part of any battle, the waiting."

He added, "As he hasn't managed to fight his way in, no doubt Ed Fyfield will hope that he'll win because we'll run out of food or water."

"And won't we?"

"Unless Ed Fyfield's people discover the pump in the lake or the pipe buried underground that supplies us, we'll have plenty of water."

"What about food?"

Whyler let out a chuckle, "I made sure we stripped every fruit bush in the area before the invasion. Unlike us, there won't be much left for Ed Fyfield's people to eat around here."

"What about our millipedes and wolves."

"They are inside the fort as well," Whyler assured me.

After a slight pause, he added, "Not that we'll have to eat our own livestock; I advanced the force shield a few minutes ago and dragged in some of the dead millipedes. We may get bored with eating millipede, but we won't starve."

"You have made sure they're dead."

"Most of them fried on the force shield," Whyler assured me. "And just to be sure, we shot each one as we dragged them in and then beheaded them. They are not going to suddenly come back to life."

Whyler patted me on the shoulder, "You've done enough for now. I'll put someone else on duty."

227

My relief arrived a few minutes later, and I went down to see Mary. I found her with a group of people huddled around a primitive wood-fired brazier that someone had made a scrap container. Thankfully, Whyler had created a small window in the force shield, and the smoke was going outside.

After I pushed my way into the huddle, Mary voiced similar thoughts to my own, "I wish I knew what would happen next. If only we knew what Ed Fyfield and his people were doing."

While we were quietly speculating, I picked up a mind-message, and I could see Ed Fyfield and some of his people sitting around a fire. As usual, there was a millipede busily roasting over it. As the cross-section of the beast was larger than the ones we had collected on North Island, I guessed that Fyfield was doing what we were doing and feasting on the millipedes that had died in battle.

At first, I couldn't work out how I could oversee Ed Fyfield, but then I realised that I was looking through Muriel's eyes and hearing what she was hearing.

As I could see water in the background, I realised that Ed Fyfield's group were down by the lake. While I was watching, Fyfield pulled out his Bowie sword and began carving up the millipede. He then began passing it around.

After eating, one of his men finally worked up the courage to ask, "So what do we do now, boss? We're trapped up here, aren't we?"

"Don't worry. We'll fly back," Fyfield replied.

"Fly back?" The man queried, "In what?"

There was a long contemptuous silence, and then Fyfield amplified, "In case you haven't noticed, the shuttle is outside the fort. It's just asking to be taken."

Someone picked up the courage to say, "And we get picked off covering the open ground."

"Not if we create a smokescreen," Fyfield replied.

"And how do we do that?"

Fyfield used one finger to indicate direction and said, "The prevailing wind is that way. So we set fire to the woods and use the smoke to cover our intentions. If we wear our survival suits, the smoke won't affect us."

After letting his plan sink in, Fyfield began carving again, but this time, instead of giving the meat to the small gathering, he placed the slices onto a large leaf, glanced at one of his men and said, "Xi Myi. We can't have our sentries going hungry, can we?"

Fyfield walked to the water's edge and started stabbing the ground. I was immediately reminded that our water supply came from the lake via a pump and a buried pipe. What if Fyfield was trying to locate it and cut us off?

I let out a sigh of relief when Fyfield stopped stabbing, went to the water's edge, and began carefully washing the blade. After drying it, he slipped it back into its scabbard.

While Fyfield had been cleaning his blade, Xi Myi had enveloped the meat he'd been given in the large leaf and set off with Muriel following behind him. A hundred metres later, Xi Myi let out a low whistle and received one in return. After handing out the meat to the first guard, he moved on and repeated the operation with the next. He moved off again and located Dugal Whiston.

Whiston spoke and ate, "So what's going on?"

Xi Myi said, "Fyfield is going to create a smokescreen. He'll capture the shuttle and fly us out of here."

Whiston smiled, "A smokescreen, 'eh?"

Xi Myi looked worried, "You were going to kill Ed Fyfield. Are you going to shoot him in the smoke?"

"Keep your voice down," Whiston snapped. He added, "I hope you are not going to say anything to Fyfield, Xi Myi."

"Don't worry," Xi Myi replied. "I'm not going to say anything; I don't like Ed Fyfield. You were the boss before Ed Fyfield turned up. If you kill him, it's good riddance as far as I'm concerned."

The next thing I was conscious of was Mary nudging me and hissing, "You've been doing that sleep writing things again."

I realised where I was; I was still by the wood-fired brazier, and everyone was staring at me. Mary said, "There's nothing to worry about; he does this quite often."

Although I was slightly annoyed that Mary had deemed it necessary to explain away my sleep-writing, I guessed that I'd embarrassed her.

Slipping my diary back into my shirt pocket, I whispered, "I'm just going to see Whyler."

"Of course you are," Mary replied, a touch of ice in her tone," I think you two are joined at the hip."

I found Whyler back in the tower, staring out at the recent battleground as if half expecting another attack at any moment.

When I told him about my latest dream, instead of seeming concerned, he looked relieved and then said, "That's a small price to pay if we get rid of him."

I must have shown surprise because Whyler said, "We don't have a way of refuelling the shuttle. And before you suggest it, we can't decant fuel from the escape pods because they use different fuel systems."

"So you intend to let Fyfield steal the shuttle?"

"If I see his men breaking cover, I intend to take down as many as I can unless they surrender," Whyler replied. "But if some of them do escape in the shuttle, it will mean that we don't have to follow them into the woods and hunt them down. If that happens, we'll take casualties for sure. If we allow Fyfield to escape on the shuttle, he is unlikely to come back."

"What about Whiston's intentions to kill Ed Fyfield?"

"Whiston's not a fool," Whyler said. "He's not going to shoot Ed Fyfield in the smoke. The shuttle will only take commands from the ship's crew. He knows this. That's why he forced me to steal the shuttle in the first place."

"So, what *will* he do?"

Whyler shrugged, "How should I know. I can only surmise."

"Surmise away," I replied.

"I think Whiston will wait until he's on the shuttle before he makes his move," Whyler replied. "From what you've just told me, Ed Fyfield is not that popular."

"So, what do we do?"

"There is nothing we can do except sit tight," Whyler replied. "If I were you, I'd get some rest. I'll have guards up here to warn us of any developments."

I was tempted to remind Whyler that all I seemed to have done since landing on Arcadia was work and sleep. Still, I decided not to because I knew he had been shouldering an enormous burden of responsibility.

Chapter Twenty-Four

Smokescreen

I awoke suddenly because Muriel and the other pterodactyls were squawking like mad. Glancing up, I realised why the noises were so strident. Muriel and her gang had flown through the smoke hole under the brazier. Some of the pterodactyls were flying around the inside of the dome, like giant moths attracted to light. Others were perched in a row on the fort's outer fencing, giving out as much sound as their lungs could provide.

While I was still looking around, Whyler appeared, tapped me on the shoulder, and nodded towards the tower. A thick fog had drifted in outside, but it wasn't normal—the water vapour smelt of burning. I caught a glimpse of flames leaping high into the sky and realised that Fyfield had carried out his intention.

As the smog continued to thicken, I glanced towards the shuttle. Although the smokescreen had yet to envelop the shuttle, I knew it wouldn't be long before it did. Glancing at Whyler, I said, "Are you seriously going to let Ed Fyfield steal the shuttle?"

"Yes," Whyler replied, "And I'm going to offer him a bit of encouragement too."

He produced a controller and pushed a button. An image of myself appeared a moment later, and it began running across the open ground outside.

My holographic appearance immediately drew fire, suggesting that Whyler's people were already inside their smokescreen and could see my image even if we could not see them.

As my hologram continued running towards the shuttle, I heard a shout, and some of Fyfield's people broke cover and began chasing my vision as if scared that I'd thwart their plans to steal the shuttle.

As more and more broke cover, I raised my stun gun, but Whyler checked me, "Let them go."

I suddenly realised the truth, "You want them to steal the shuttle, don't you?"

"Correct," Whyler replied. "Without fuel, the shuttle is of no real use to us, and if they take it, they should leave us alone."

As we watched, white-clad figures began jumping into the shuttle. Whyler waited until the last person had jumped on board and then produced another controller and triggered it.

In response, the outer door of the shuttle slammed shut, and then the machine took off. As it disappeared into the smog that Fyfield had created, Whyler said, "Once the fire burns itself out, we will have to organise search parties. We will need to check that none of Fyfield's people has been left behind. If there are any left, they could cause us trouble."

~*~

It was nearly three hours before the smog started to clear, and our search party cautiously ventured out, half expecting to end up in a shooting match. When nothing happened, we all breathed a sigh of relief.

Although the fires had largely died down by that time, there were still pockets of glowing embers. As we moved through the village, I was pleased to note that most of the houses under construction had sustained very little damage despite the escape pods crashing down close by. Even the burning embers that had fallen from the sky didn't appear to have done any harm.

The forests were another matter. I was amazed at just how much of the forest had been destroyed by Fyfield's people. Then, we realised why. The smell of accelerant in some locations indicated just how determined Ed Fyfield had been to start the blaze.

As we began tramping through the charred remains of the forest, we came upon twelve human bodies and at least fifty Arcadian millipedes, but we realised that they had all died before the fire started. A sense of guilt settled on me. Although my dreams indicated that Ed Fyfield wanted me dead, helping to kill so many of the opposition made me feel uncomfortable. Although we were on another planet, we'd brought Earth's killing disease with us.

Eventually, we came upon the escape pods that had landed long before Ed Fyfield's people had dropped in on us. As the forest in that area had not been burnt down, and there was no evidence of recent human activity, Whyler was on the point of calling off the search when I heard the crackle of breaking twigs, and Muriel sent me mind image of people waiting to ambush us.

I dived sideways, shouting, "Get down."

As I hit the burnt forest floor, I expected to feel gun-blasts passing overhead, but instead, I just heard someone shout out, "Don't shoot! Don't shoot!"

Glancing up, I saw Xi Myi and three other men emerging from the unburnt section of the forest with their hands held high.

As I climbed to my feet again, Whyler moved in and said, "Are there any more of you?"

Xi Myi shook his head, "Just us. The rest were going to steal the shuttle."

After telling them to come out of cover, Whyler said, "Why didn't you go with Ed Fyfield and the others?"

"The fires cut us off when the wind direction changed," Xi Myi replied.

After instructing Xi Myi and his gang to step forward, Whyler ensured they had been disarmed and ordered everyone to head back to our village.

As I'd seen Xi Myi in my dreams, I deliberately fell into step beside him and said, "Did Dugal Whiston go with the rest?"

Xi gave me a surprised glance and echoed, "Go with the rest?"

As I didn't want to disclose my dream skills, I said, "We had bugs in the woods, and I saw and heard you talking to Dugal Whiston. Whiston was going to go with Ed Fyfield when he stole the shuttle. So did Whiston go with Fyfield?"

Xi nodded, "As far as I know, yes."

"What was Fyfield going to do with the Shuttle?"

"He was going to fly the shuttle to the Fyfield Valley and show it off to the Great Ones," Xi replied. "He's going to use it to collect salvage from the wreck if it's safe."

I was tempted to mention the broken fuel gauge but didn't bother because there was no point. It was Fyfield who had stolen the shuttle and not Xi.

Once we were back in the village, Xi and the others were interrogated; they all disliked Ed Fyfield and swiftly decided to switch sides.

Chapter Twenty-Five

More Dreams from Akbar

Usually, Akbar's dreams involved either the present or the future, but his next dream was different. It was looking back and seemed like a faded photograph in my mind.

I saw Whyler searching the shuttle. After what seemed like an eternity, Whyler let out a whoop of delight and held up a small chip that had been hiding in the shuttle's heavily upholstered headliner. He placed the chip in the device he'd shown me, began tapping keys, and then replaced the chip in the exact location he'd found it.

Even though I was back in my dreamworld, questions bubbled to the surface. During our flights to the wreck, the Trojan chip had been a significant problem. I was surprised that Whyler hadn't mentioned the find to me or told me why he put it back. While I was still thinking about the implications of what I'd dream-witnessed, Whyler's image faded from my mind and was replaced by a new sequence.

I saw Ed Fyfield's people clambering into the shuttle a moment later.

Then someone shouted, "Where is he?"

"Where's who?"

"Bee Bee," a voice called out, "He came in here. Search for him."

While questions concerning my whereabouts were being bandied about, pandemonium broke out as the outer doors shut, and the shuttle took off without warning.

Ed Fyfield shouted for calm and told his followers that there was nothing to worry about because he's programmed the shuttle to land in the Fyfield Valley. Despite Ed Fyfield's comments, I sensed that something was wrong.

After flying on the shuttle, I had learned to read the engine sounds. As the shuttle continued to rise, worry lines formed on Ed Fyfield's brow, and he dashed towards the control console and attempted to take manual control, but the machine continued to climb. As the shuttle continued on its journey, I knew where it was going. And I knew why.

Whyler had reprogrammed the Trojan to take Ed Fyfield to the Wreck. Once the passengers on the shuttle realised that they had returned to the wreck, the recriminations started.

The third dream showed Ed Fyfield interrogating the ship's computer to locate additional fuel. When he realised that any available fuel had already been taken by Whyler, Fyfield flew into a rage.

It didn't take the other long to realise what was going on, and pandemonium broke out again.

Fyfield attempted to calm the crowd by telling them that he'd located an un-launched escape pod and that he could get them back to Arcadia. After telling everyone to activate their survival suits again, Fyfield led them down a series of passages. Eventually, Fyfield led them until they came to an escape bay and true to his word, there was a pod waiting for them.

As they began climbing in, most of the would-be escapees removed their breathing masks. I recognised the man I used to call Dad. I stared at one of the men who hadn't released their masks. Although only his eyes were visible, I realised it was Dugal Whiston.

After Fyfield had punched in the landing coordinates, the escape pod disengaged from the wreck and began its descent to Arcadia.

After slight buffeting as the pod hit Arcadia's atmosphere, it began moving towards the Fyfield Valley. I saw Ed Fyfield visibly relaxed and then turned in his seat, "There, we have nothing to worry about."

At that point, Dugal Whiston made his move. After pulling off his mask, Whiston said, "Your hair-brained scheme cost the lives of twelve people."

Ed Fyfield swung around and glared at Whiston, "What are you doing here?"

"I thought I'd join you and see how your operation panned out," Whiston replied. "And as I said, your hair-brained scheme cost the lives of twelve people."

Ed Fyfield responded by springing out of his chair and moving towards Whiston with his Bowie sword at the ready. Whiston responded by hastily retreating, but as he continued to back away, he said, "So you're going to kill me, eh?"

Fyfield answered with a grin and carried on advancing. Whiston waited until Fyfield was only a few metres away and then pulled out a pistol and fired twice in swift succession. Fyfield flinched and moved in fast and attempted to skewer Whiston on his sword, but his opponent dodged the thrust and fired again.

The third shot left a neat hole in Fyfield's chest but didn't appear to have much effect because Fyfield attempted to stab Whiston again. After ducking and diving and firing again, Whiston stumbled and fell to the floor. Fyfield moved in fast and drove his sword straight through Whiston's body. As Whiston croaked and then collapsed to the floor, Fyfield glanced around and said, "Self-defence. Right!"

Instead of giving an answer, everyone just stared at Fyfield open-mouthed. He'd taken four bullets but was still standing.

Fyfield repeated, "It was self-defence. Right!"

This time the whole assembly called back, "Yeah. Self-defence."

After pulling his Bowie sword out of Whiston's body and carefully wiping the blade on Whiston's environmental suit, Fyfield began walking back to his seat. Partway there, he staggered and began examining his wounds. He let out two blood filled coughs before collapsing to the floor. One or two people rushed towards the bodies but swiftly realised that both men were dead.

As the would-be paramedics began backing away, I caught a glimpse of the man I used to call Dad. His face looked smug.

Then, I realised why. Before Whiston and Ed Fyfield turned up, Suzanna and himself had been accepted by the Great ones as the group leaders. As his two rivals had just killed one another, the status quo would probably be restored.

Realising that showing pleasure at the deaths would not go down well, my former Dad's demeanour changed, and he said, "A terrible thing has just happened. Can I suggest that Dugal Whiston and Ed Fyfield's deaths be recorded as having died in combat fighting for the Great Ones rather than the real truth coming out?"

After a few seconds, a murmur of agreement ran around the shuttle. The two deaths would be brushed under the carpet.

Chapter Twenty-Six

Back at the Village

I didn't discuss my latest dreams with Whyler for several days. In the first place, I couldn't believe that he'd deliberately allowed Ed Fyfield to steal the shuttle, knowing he'd probably be stranded on the wreck. The second reason was that I breathed a sigh of relief when Dugal Whiston and Ed Fyfield died.

It was a problem that I needed to wrestle with. On the one hand, the three acts appeared indefensible, yet being rid of Whiston and Fyfield seemed to benefit all.

As avoiding Whyler for a while seemed a sensible thing to do, I joined a group of volunteers and began the process of turning the burnt ground into fields. There didn't seem many points of allowing it to return to nature.

Mary didn't go with me because she'd been sick. I have to confess I am worried about Mary. She's been ill several times this week.

Printed in Great Britain
by Amazon